Hackneyed Tales

Hackneyed Tales

Andy Boca

This is a work of fiction. Names, characters, places, and incidents either are the product of the author's imagination or are used fictitiously. Any resemblance to actual persons, living or dead, events, or locales is entirely coincidental.

Copyright © 2022 by Andy Boca

All rights reserved. No part of this book may be reproduced or used in any manner without written permission of the copyright owner except for the use of quotations in a book review.

First paperback edition

ISBNs
Paperback: 978-1-80227-647-3
eBook: 978-1-80227-648-0

Acknowledgements

A big thank you to my friend Leon Mills, who was the first person to see any of these stories and provided invaluable feedback and analysis.

* * *

A special thanks to the following people in the ALFOS family for their encouragement:

Alice Palace	Linda Mills
Cheryl Robinson	Marilia Stagkouraki
Chris Sweet	Mark Ward
Chris & Jennifer Williams	Michael Greenfield
Clare Williams	Richie Rundle
Drew Lawson	Sarah Ryan
Garry Wallace	Sean Johnston
Gavin Richards	Simon Ewins
Hannah Mortimer	Stefan Oliver
James & Tina Davidson	Tina Jones
Liam Stenhouse	Tristan Llewellyn

In Loving Memory of Andrew Weatherall

For Linda
For believing

The trouble with fiction is that it's all made up.

Anonymous

Contents

Acknowledgements................................... v

For The Love of Dog 1
Cycle Path Encounter................................ 8
Will The Grass Ever Be Greener?..................... 14
Saving Grace 23
Gran's Scheme of Things 31
Not A Prostitute You Know 46
Time Wasted 58
Got To Score 69
Love At First Bite 79
Nicker In A Twist................................... 89
Tunnel Vision....................................... 99
1940.. 110
7 O'Clock Drop...................................... 120
Recapture The Thrill................................ 132
Pawn Hub 142
Kiss Goodbye To All That 155
Possessions 167
This Used To Be Paradise Row 178
Reservoir Decalogues................................ 188
Trial And Error 199
Shed.. 210

For The Love of Dog

Harriet had never been to a dog wedding before and as she always hated letting other people down, she politely accepted the invitation; even going so far as to say she was really looking forward to it. This was despite not having the foggiest idea what to expect. Or even the doggiest idea, Harriet laughed to herself, and then wished that there was somebody around to share that with. Presumably, Harriet thought, it will be like any other wedding she'd been to, though perhaps without the awful disco and hopefully, she wouldn't end up having a drunken one-night stand with some complete stranger which she would then regret for many months to come.

"No, I'm not doing anything else," Harriet said to herself. "I need to take every opportunity I'm offered to get out there and meet people again." She was lucky she knew a few nice people who would occasionally enquire after her. Sometimes they might even invite her to meet up and join them, just as long as other single people were going to be there as well.

Assuming this wouldn't be too formal an affair, Harriet dressed smartly but casually on the morning of the big day and hoped that she wouldn't be the only person not wearing a hat. As she walked the fifteen minutes it took to get to Clissold Park, where the ceremony was being held, she sensed that a feeling of romance was definitely in the air. Not just canine romance, but romance for all animals everywhere. Perhaps it was that first day of spring feeling she experienced once a year. It was hard to tell as it varied drastically from one year to the next, a bit like Easter, and it didn't happen on a specific date like Christmas, or her birthday, both of which were days she now dreaded.

The sun was shining, and Harriet felt confident that she was going to have an enjoyable day and once again reminded herself that she wasn't actually missing anything else by doing this. It could definitely be a lot worse. She might well be stuck in her flat on a nice sunny day like this or just walking around the park aimlessly, in both cases, wishing she wasn't all alone.

Harriet entered the park she now knew so well and made her way towards the trees, just to the right of the defunct swimming pool, where she'd been told the ceremony was going to take place. In the distance she could make out a small group of people attaching a purple ribbon to two adjacent trees. The ribbon was neither long enough nor taut enough for a person to do that tightrope walking thing which she'd noticed had recently become very popular in the park, so she assumed she was heading in the right direction.

"Ah, Harriet," said a lady called Rosemary, as Harriet arrived, "so pleased you could make it."

"Not at all, thanks for inviting me. I'm really very excited," Harriet replied, realising as she said this that she was being totally honest, without actually knowing the reason why.

"I'm not sure you know everybody here," said Rosemary, before proceeding to introduce Harriet to five other people, none of whom she had met before.

Four of these were women of a much older age than Harriet, and whose names she didn't quite catch, while the fifth person was a man called Geoff, or Jeff, who appeared to be in the same age group as her. Harriet wondered if it would make any difference if the man was called Jeff or Geoff and decided that yes, it probably would. She was evidently being set up as part of some matchmaking here, she thought. It was obvious. Rosemary already had a husband and all the other guests, apart from this man, were older women. Maybe she'd been right all along about romance being in the air. Harriet studied the man a little more closely, being as discreet as she possibly could. Her first impressions were favourable. He appeared clean and was tidily dressed in a pair of blue chinos and a plain light blue shirt and wasn't as flabby as some men of his age she'd seen. Harriet had long resigned herself that any man she would meet now would come under the category of damaged goods. Then there was the added conundrum that, even if she was accepting of someone, they also had to show a modicum of interest in her.

"So, are you local as well, Harriet?" asked the man.

This was definitely a good start, thought Harriet. Not only did he remember her name, but he was also showing an immediate interest in her.

"Yes, do you know Albion Road, just off Green Lanes, before you get to Newington Green?"

"Not personally," he replied. "But I know exactly where you mean. That isn't too far from me."

"Excellent!" Harriet exclaimed, before realising that that might have come across as being a somewhat inappropriate response and could possibly be construed as being a bit too keen. She decided she'd better talk to the other guests for a little while before she said something that would ruin any chances she had with this man and would concentrate on the wedding in hand for the time being.

"So, who are the happy couple?" Harriet said, turning herself towards the women present who were now attaching various pieces of bunting to the purple ribbon.

"Douglas and Cleopatra," said Rosemary, pointing in turn to the two dogs also present amongst the gathering, neither of which, fortunately, appeared to be showing any signs of pre-nuptial nerves. "Cleopatra is Joan's dog and has taken a real shine to my Douglas over the past few weeks. They've become completely inseparable," continued Rosemary.

"Absolutely." Joan concurred and smiled revealing some oddly shaped teeth.

"And what make are they?" asked Harriet.

"I assume you mean breed," replied Rosemary, rolling her eyes. "In which case, Douglas is a Labrador and Cleopatra is a Beagle."

"Ah, proper real dogs then," said Hariet. "That's nice, because these days all you hear about are Cockapoos, Yorkie Doodles and Jack Shihtz. Why can't people just admit that they're all a load of mongrels and be done with it?"

"Well, we're not planning on inventing another breed, just yet," said Rosemary, smiling.

"So, this isn't a shotgun wedding then?" Harriet laughed, a little louder than was strictly necessary.

"Definitely not. They are head over heels in love," said Joan, giving Harriet a proud smile.

Harriet smiled back, looked at the two dogs, and decided that they could very well be described as being in love. A horrible thought crossed her mind that perhaps nobody had ever really loved her because, as far as she could recall, nobody had ever asked, or even tried, to sniff her bottom. Maybe she had never really been in love with anybody either. She was fairly sure that there was nobody who she had thought she'd been in love with, whose bottom she would have wanted to sniff. Perhaps Brian's, if push came to shove. Brian was the man she'd been most upset about when they'd split up and had taken the longest time to get over. Maybe that's how you know when you truly love somebody and are ready to get married - when you wouldn't think twice about sniffing that person's bottom. Either, if asked, or just spontaneously on a whim.

The wedding went smoothly, and Douglas and Cleopatra were pronounced dog and wife.

"That was lovely. What now?" asked Harriet.

"I need to get Douglas home," replied Rosemary. "I think he's had quite enough excitement for one day."

"Same here, we'll walk back with you," said Joan, attaching a lead to Cleopatra's harness and dragging her away.

The other three women nodded in agreement and started to dismantle the bunting and purple ribbon from the trees, until there wasn't a single trace of there ever having been any kind of wedding in that particular spot. Apart from, Harriet noticed, a small turd that one of the dogs had left behind. Harriet was no expert, but she assumed it was impossible to determine whether it was Douglas or Cleopatra who had been the culprit, but she did know that perhaps she might have been wrong earlier about there being no signs of any pre-marital nerves. Harriet wondered if anybody else was aware of this and if not, would it be the correct protocol to mention it? She decided against saying anything, just in case it ruined the whole ambience of the occasion.

* * *

Harriet awoke the following morning, hungover and alone, as usual. Unable to get out of bed, she attempted to run the events of the previous day over in her mind. Alarmingly, there were a number of large gaps, and she wondered if these could be significant in any way. Perhaps they would come back to her in due course over the following days and weeks.

    Geoff or Jeff, something else she couldn't remember, or was possibly too scared to want to find out, agreed to come for a drink with her after the wedding. They joked about it being the wedding reception. The sunny weather had continued long into the afternoon, and they sat outside in the Clissold Park Tavern's beer garden, drinking and laughing well into the evening, hardly noticing the light fading to darkness. They moved inside when they finally became aware that the temperature had dropped.

    It was very possible that they'd continued to drink until they were told that the pub was closing. The obvious thing to do would be to carry on drinking, as they were having such a wonderful time. They walked the short distance back to her flat, picking up a bottle of wine from the 24-hour shop on the way. Harriet recalled that they'd held hands all the way back and how wonderful that had felt. In that brief moment, she'd no longer felt alone and unloved, and was with somebody who wasn't ashamed to be seen with her and who was also enjoying her company.

    Harriet had gone to the bathroom to freshen up as soon as they'd arrived back at her flat and considered it a good idea to come out of there completely naked. It had been a long time since a man had been in her home and she didn't want to prematurely lose him. She remembered calling out his name in what she hoped was a husky, sexy voice, while trying to seductively walk towards him. Harriet had then, unintentionally, fallen down the small flight of stairs and landed in a crumpled heap at the intrigued man's feet. Fortunately, she'd quickly managed to pick herself back up again, almost as if nothing had happened. Harriet had then taken the seemingly unperturbed Geoff/Jeff by the hand and led him in the direction of her bedroom. She had knelt on the bed on all fours and decided that she would optimistically stick her bottom in the air, whilst simultaneously trying to prepare herself for the inevitable disappointment that this was yet another man who did not truly love her and want to marry her.

Oh well, thought Harriet, another typical wedding, but at least there hadn't been an awful disco to contend with. She started to cry, quite slowly at first, before her whole body began to convulse as she sobbed uncontrollably. Maybe this time, she hoped, it might make her feel a little better.

Cycle Path Encounter

David had woken up unusually early for a Saturday and decided to use the situation to his advantage. He needed to do some serious shopping at the big supermarket. If he went soon, he could get it all over and done with by eight in the morning, freeing up the rest of the day to do whatever he wanted to. He would decide exactly what that was going to be once he had finished his shopping. He truly believed that it was always best to focus on just one chore at a time.

He opened the fridge and surveyed the hopeless situation. Although there were quite a lot of things in there, they were either past their best before date or would never get eaten. He cleared out everything, leaving a completely empty fridge just waiting to be filled with wonderful, new, delicious items. It felt like a new beginning.

David set off on the twenty-minute walk to the supermarket, feeling quite excited at the prospect of filling his empty fridge. He had brought two large bags for life with him, and anyone who by chance saw these, would know at once that he definitely meant business. The sun was just coming up and David thought about how much he loved the sunrise. I really should make more of an effort to see it every day, he thought, I just wish it didn't happen so frustratingly early and cause me to miss it. Perhaps I could look into which places had a sunrise that started around a couple of hours later than here and go and live there. Then I really would be able to fully appreciate it after hopefully, having had a good night's sleep, and could take in the full splendour of the occasion while enjoying a good breakfast and the first cup of coffee of the day.

Anyway, he was experiencing it today and it only enhanced his already joyful mood. As he passed Clissold Park, he was amazed at how beautiful it looked. Even better than usual. Possibly, because it was virtually deserted, and everywhere looked better when there were no other people around. From now on, he would get up this early every morning, he decided.

There were only a couple of other shoppers in the supermarket when David arrived, and it almost felt like he had the whole place to himself. There was no need to rush as he would normally do when it was busy. Today, he would use a trolley rather than a basket, and take his time to examine everything available, just to make sure he wasn't missing out on any products he had previously been unaware of.

The smell of recently baked bread immediately attracted him to the bakery department. He couldn't quite believe how much was on display. Usually, when he went shopping there were only a few loaves of bread left, and these generally involved something or other made with cranberries, which David was not a big fan of. He read all the labels, satisfying himself that he was now a lot more knowledgeable about bread than he had ever been before. After some careful deliberation, he opted for his bread of choice saying "San Francisco Style Sourdough" out loud, in what he assumed was a passable west coast American accent.

Although David had never been to San Francisco, he now felt safe in the knowledge that he would soon know what the sourdough bread was like in that spectacular city. If by chance, he ever got to meet anybody from San Francisco he could now reliably have a conversation with them about their famous bread. When they would say something like 'Gee David, the sourdough bread we have back home in Frisco is to die for.' He would reply 'You bet your bottom it is, Brad. It's awesome.' It suddenly occurred to him though, that he hadn't actually tried the sourdough bread yet. He would therefore have to wait until he got home and hope that he didn't meet anybody called Brad from San Francisco in the meantime. If he did, he would try and steer the conversation away from bread on the whole, and sourdough in particular.

This behaviour continued in the same vein for the rest of David's shopping adventure, and by the time he arrived at the checkout, his trolley was full of exciting items he couldn't wait to get home and try. David had also made quite a few new potential friends who he would now be confident enough to freely converse with on the subject of their traditional speciality foods, if he was ever lucky enough to meet them in real life.

At that precise moment, David didn't feel quite so excluded just because he hadn't travelled to any exotic countries. He would soon be the proud owner of a number of sensational products, and each one was now one less thing he hadn't previously discovered from a place he hadn't yet visited.

Even though David had spent more time than ever before in a supermarket, the streets were still pleasantly quiet when he came outside. He had filled both of his bags for life, and there was something of a swagger about him that is often found in people who have already achieved the main task they had set out to do that day, by the morning.

Although both bags were heavy, David felt perfectly balanced, and set off on his walk home compiling a mental list of the foods he would try out first. He walked along the empty pavement, which was alongside an equally unoccupied cycle lane, which was part of the unusually clear road. What a beautiful morning, thought David. I can't wait to get home and fix breakfast. He

Cycle Path Encounter

had already decided that he would try the sourdough first and therefore, carried on with the Americanisms for the time being.

'Yes, I'll fix breakfast, then I'll grab me some brunch, then I'll have me some lunch. Are you trying to break my chops, David? That's way too many meals you douchebag. Sorry, my bad. How many goddamn meals is that David, you schmuck? I don't know you bozo, you do the math. I haven't got time to bust my balls here. I need to try and speak to Samantha to see if she's changed her mind this week and wants to be my friend again. And then she could help me eat all this food and we would always be happy. Way to go!' continued David, who was now really getting into the swing of things.

David's reverie was rudely interrupted by the sound of a bell, loud enough to give him the impression that it was directly behind him. The startled David leaped to one side, narrowly avoiding a man who went hurtling past him on a bicycle. "Hey! Don't ring your bell at me," said David.

The cyclist, who was now just a little way ahead of David, instantly stopped his bicycle and turned his head towards David. "What did you say?"

David, who had now also stopped and had put down his two heavy bags for life, replied, "I said will you please not ring your bell at me. This is a pavement."

"What's your problem you fucking weirdo?" said the cyclist.

"My problem is that I don't want you ringing your bell at me when I'm on the pavement. Why don't you use the cycle lane or even the road?"

"Don't tell me what to do," said the cyclist, now manoeuvering his bicycle so that both he and his precious possession were facing David. As soon as he had completed this action, the cyclist began to imagine himself as Sir Galahad, his favourite of all the Knights of the Round Table, sitting proudly upon his trusty steed.

David was now starting to get quite flustered. He'd been having such a good morning and was feeling the happiest he had felt in weeks, and now this man was spoiling everything. He took a couple of steps towards the cyclist and continued to put forward his case. "You could have easily gone past me, even on the pavement, without ringing your bell. Just because you've got a bell doesn't mean you have to ring it, you know? But you shouldn't be on the pavement, anyway. Pavements are for people to walk on, not for bikes to ride on. Especially as there is a cycle lane and a road, which, as you can very clearly see, are both completely empty."

While David was saying all of this, the cyclist was staring at him, as if David was totally insane, and said, "You're fucking mad, do you know that?"

"Me, mad? I'm not the one riding on the pavement, am I? Why can't you understand that?" replied David.

The cyclist at this point decided to carefully place his cherished bicycle flat down on the pavement. "Are you calling me stupid, you fucking nobhead?"

"Look, please, you're ruining my day. Can you please just leave me alone, please. Can't you just go to wherever it is you want to go to? If you're in that much of a hurry that you have to ring your bell at me, why have you stopped now?" enquired David.

The cyclist obviously never had an answer to David's perfectly logical question as he made no attempt to respond verbally. Instead, he charged towards David and struck him with a powerful punch to the side of his head. The force of the blow knocked David backwards, causing him to fall crashing into his bags for life prior to landing flat out on the hard stone pavement.

Cycle Path Encounter

David first heard a sickening cracking sound. To his horror, this was quickly followed by a pungent odour that appeared to be emanating from the now damp bottom half of his horizontal body. While it was impossible for David to be absolutely certain, he had a dreadful feeling that it was the 'Indian Starter Selection for Two' along with the 'Vietnamese style Bún bò Huế', that had been completely destroyed.

David sat up slowly and stared, bewildered by the carnage all around him. His head hung limply, and with his lifeless legs spread apart, he resembled a discarded man-sized rag doll. The cyclist, still seething, stood aggressively over David, but was taken aback when David began to cry. This wasn't just the typical weeping, or even sobbing, that one might expect from a dejected man who now suspects that a significant proportion of his recently purchased groceries may have been damaged beyond repair. Instead, David was releasing a terrifying sound, one which had been lying dormant within the darkest depths of his violated mind. A sound that shocked even the cyclist. It was almost as if David was using every single ounce of strength in his body to produce these blood-curdling screams.

The cyclist began walking backwards, while staring at the slumped figure who was still howling with all his might. "There's something wrong with you, mate. You need help," he said, before getting back on to his bicycle and riding away.

Through his streaming tears, David noticed that the man was still cycling on the pavement. He then tried to fathom out why he could hear a cry of what sounded very much like "Giddy up!" coming from way off in the distance.

Will The Grass Ever Be Greener?

Robert closed his front door and stepped out into the grey mist. He was about to go on his favourite walk. Although it usually took him exactly twenty-seven minutes from door to door, he always had a worrying feeling that something might happen which would delay him. Even though, in eight years of doing the same walk, sometimes two, three or four times a month, nothing ever had.

Robert pulled up his scarf to protect him from the cold and looked at his watch. It was eighteen minutes past two in the afternoon. He would arrive at his destination at two forty-five, a full fifteen minutes before kick-off. It would then take six frustrating minutes to get through the security check outside. Allowing four minutes to walk up the stairs two at a time and get through the crowded concourse, would see him reach his designated seat in the stadium just as the two teams were about to come out on to the pitch. He always felt a satisfying sense of relief that everything had gone according to plan and, once again, he wasn't going to miss anything crucial he might regret for the rest of his life.

Robert took his usual route, which he trusted to be the quickest. Through Clissold Park, then pretty much straight all the way until he arrived at his turnstile entrance. He had been doing this journey ever since he'd bought his flat those eight years ago and didn't have to think too much about where he was going. This normally freed up his mind, enabling him to devote all his thoughts to the forthcoming game. This Saturday afternoon, though, was different.

No matter how much Robert tried to concentrate on the approaching game, he was unable to ignore the problem that had been nagging him for the past month. How was he going to tell Lisa that he didn't want her living with him anymore? Robert had made the decision back in December, but in order not to ruin anyone's Christmas & New Year celebrations, especially his own, he'd postponed any horrible, miserable stuff until well after the holiday season was over. He had now gone a further four weeks without doing anything, and it was starting to have a negative effect on him.

He wasn't sleeping very well and had been waking up at least twenty minutes before his alarm was programmed to go off. He couldn't fully concentrate at work and now it was even interfering with the football. Something needed to be done and done quickly. He decided he would do it this weekend, whatever happened. Actually, if we win, I'll enjoy my Saturday and do it tomorrow. If we lose, I'll do it tonight and get it over and done with, Robert told himself, optimistically anticipating a straightforward home victory against Burnley. Robert congratulated himself on his great idea. I will leave it to fate, or to The Arsenal at any rate. We should win and, if we do, I'll go home happy. Maybe go for a few pints with Lisa, go for a curry together, somewhere local, even have a last bunk up with her before telling her it's all over late on Sunday morning. Although, thought Robert, we haven't been having too many of those recently, realizing the same applied to both home wins and bunk ups. That was part of the problem, he would have to tell her, not the only thing of course, but, once your girlfriend starts turning you down for sex on a regular basis, you've got to start questioning where the relationship is heading.

Robert continued his journey, a little more relaxed about the impending predicament being resolved this weekend, although he was still not able to fully concentrate on what he would like to, which was how he anticipated the game going. His mind wandered back to the beginning of the relationship.

Robert had met Lisa seven months ago at a funeral. They had got on well enough for Robert to suggest, exactly three months later, that she move in with him. Lisa had seemed overjoyed at his suggestion. At the time, she was temporarily sleeping on a friend's sofa, so this meant that she was able to move into his place straight away. Robert, whose profession was Head of Human Resources at an I.T. Company, had joked that Lisa had passed her probationary period and that he was therefore, now willing to take her on permanently. Lisa carried on with the role playing, saying that she, consequently, would have to give him a month's notice if she was leaving him, whereas he would have to give her a verbal warning followed by two written ones before he could get rid of her.

"Not unless you have been found guilty of gross misconduct, then its instant dismissal," Robert had said, with a deadly serious look on his face which had taken Lisa by surprise. Lisa had left it at that and then went very quiet, he now remembered.

As Robert made his way towards his desired destination, he began to review Lisa's qualities over in his mind once again. He liked Lisa a lot, most of the time, but he wasn't sure he would ever fall in love with her. Lisa was certainly quite attractive and had a decent body but, if the truth be told, she was never going to win Miss World or even Miss Stoke Newington. They didn't have a great deal in common, either. Lisa wasn't interested in football and there were musical differences, as well. He loved classic seventies rock, whereas Lisa, who was a fair bit younger than him, preferred the music of the nineties and noughties. Her favourites seemed to be solo artists like Alanis Morisette, Bjork, and Franz Ferdinand. All three of them were terrible but the bloke was the worst of the lot. He could clearly remember the expression on Lisa's face after she'd played him her favourite track of his, 'Take Me Out'. All he could say to her was, "He definitely needs to be taken out alright. Somebody needs to shoot that bohemian bender and make the world a much better place." He liked watching action and adventure films, while Lisa preferred these Scandinavian murder mysteries with subtitles. The last one he'd watched with her involved some blind detective who liked to play the oboe or the bassoon, or something like that, to help him solve a case. On top of this, now that the sex had dried up as well, it seemed the obvious solution would be to call it a day and go their separate ways.

A murky fog had started to descend, and Robert had only noticed how serious it was once he reached the top of Avenell Road. At this part of his journey, he always instinctively looked over to his right, towards where the old ground used to be. Robert could barely make out the retained façade of the once beautiful Highbury Stadium which had now been converted into luxury flats.

The memory of Robert's first ever game at Highbury flashed into his mind. He could vividly recall being a nine-year-old little boy, holding his grandfather's hand as they walked up the grey stone steps, and along the narrow concourse towards their seats in the West Stand Lower Tier. His first glimpse of the pitch and how amazed he'd been at how green the grass appeared to be. The way it stood out against the surrounding stands, almost making them look drab in comparison. The way his grandfather had just let Robert experience it all for himself, knowing that there wasn't any need to say or point anything out to him. Robert remembered looking up, wide-eyed and open-mouthed, and will never forget the look of recognition he saw on his grandfather's smiling face.

Highbury had meant so much to Robert, and he was one of the few people who had shown little enthusiasm for the move back in 2006. We should never have left Highbury, he reiterated in his mind. We were on the verge of something really big during those last few years there. Leaving our home and moving to a new stadium ruined all of that, and it doesn't look like its coming back for a while either. Sometimes, the grass isn't always greener on the other side.

The fog was getting thicker, and Robert felt like it was pressing down on him. It wasn't quite at the pea-souper proportions he recalled from when he was a child, but he was now finding it difficult to see more than a few feet in front of him. Robert arrived at the turnstile entrance and a look at his watch confirmed that he was right on schedule. What he hadn't anticipated though, were the large crowds of people gathered outside. It was impossible to know where to join the queue for the security check. He overheard somebody say that they weren't letting anybody in at the moment, and it certainly didn't help matters when even more people continued to arrive. Robert stood waiting impatiently along with everybody else.

"They can't play in this. Every cunt here can see fuck all," shouted somebody.

"Who said that?" somebody else shouted, to widespread laughter.

"I wish this fog would fuck off," shouted another person, to further laughter.

"Who said that?" shouted a different person to the one who had previously shouted it, but this time nobody laughed. Then people started singing because they didn't know what else to do.

A short while later, after there had been no improvement in the situation, there was an official announcement transmitted to the large crowd outside. "Ladies & Gentlemen, Boys and Girls. Can I have your attention, please? Due to unforeseen circumstances beyond Arsenal Football Club's control, we regret to advise you that the referee, in the interest of paramount safety, has decided to postpone today's match against Burnley Football Club until a later date. Please check for further announcements on our website and in the media. Arsenal Football Club would like to wish you all a safe journey home and thank you for your understanding in this matter. Arsenal Football Club would also like to thank you for your continued support, and we look forward to seeing you all back here again very soon."

"Who said that?" shouted the person who had originally shouted it. There was some initial laughter, but this was soon drowned out by the sound of people booing. Nobody, it seemed, could muster up the enthusiasm for any singing.

Robert, along with thousands of other disappointed people, started to make his way home. His thoughts soon turned to what he was going to do about telling Lisa that their relationship was over. His plan of leaving it up to Arsenal to decide when he was going to do it had failed, although he did still favour the Sunday option. I know Arsenal didn't win, he decided, but they didn't lose either. He realized he hadn't made any provisions for the possibility of a draw, but quickly dismissed this as an irrelevance. Although it was true that neither team had won, it definitely hadn't been a draw.

He would gauge Lisa's reaction to his early return to determine when he should have the uncomfortable conversation. If she was pleased to see him, then he would wait until Sunday. If, on the other hand, he detected an impassive attitude from her, he would get it done and dusted, there and then.

Even though he was sure that this was what he wanted, he was still dreading the whole process. What if Lisa doesn't agree, in the same way that he does, about this being a good idea? What if she takes the news really badly? What if she starts smashing things up? His things, in his flat, that is. What if she starts crying? Or worse, starts screaming. What if she tries to kill herself? Or worse still, tries to kill him? She was already slowly killing him as it is, what with all this worry about how he was going to break the news to her, and how she would react to being told to leave his flat and go and find somewhere else to live. If not immediately, then at least within the week.

As he walked home, Robert felt as if his entire body was absorbing the enclosing fog, and he was overcome by a strange feeling of sadness. Perhaps it would be easier all round if he just left things the way they were, he thought. It wasn't as if Lisa had done anything wrong. Sure, things could be a lot better, but he wasn't that unhappy, was he? Maybe this is all part of some mid-life crisis he was going through. He knew lots of people who began acting strangely when they got to his age. Some bought electric scooters or roller skates, while others started using Grecian 2000 and contemplated having an affair.

While he had so far resisted all of these temptations, Robert began to wonder whether this was his reaction to a mid-life crisis. Evicting somebody, only four months after asking them to move in with him, simply because he thought he could do a lot better. He decided that he would at least give Lisa a chance to save their relationship. They would talk it over amicably and do their best to make it work. These days, people just don't try hard enough. Where's the loyalty? Where's the commitment? They're all too quick to take what they can and then move on to try and find something which they think will be preferable.

Robert arrived home, relieved to be out of the cold, and with a clearer mind than when he'd left earlier that afternoon. There was no sign of Lisa, either in the living room or the kitchen. Further down the hallway there appeared to be an unusual sound coming from the bedroom. He decided to approach quietly and on tiptoe made his way towards the bedroom door. By now it was clearly apparent that somebody was in an advanced state of sexual gratification. There was no way he could be certain, but he assumed it must be Lisa. There didn't appear to be any other sound coming from somebody else. Momentarily confused, Robert tried to make sense of what was happening. Was Lisa pleasuring herself in there? Did she do this a lot when he went to football? Why couldn't she have waited until he got home?

"Oh yes, yes." Robert heard coming from the other side of the door.

Robert pressed his ear right up to the door, feeling quite aroused now as he imagined Lisa on the other side. He wondered if Lisa usually spoke out loud to herself when she was on her own in this situation.

"Oh, yes, yes, that's so good."

Still unable to detect anything other than Lisa's voice, Robert decided that yes, she probably did.

"Oh, babe yes, yes, keep doing that to me You're going to make come in a minute."

Hearing this, Robert now had an inkling that perhaps Lisa was not alone after all.

He slowly opened the bedroom door. Lisa was lying naked on the bed and his suspicions were confirmed when he saw that there was somebody else with her. He couldn't quite recognize who exactly, as whoever it was, had their face buried between Lisa's thighs.

"What the fuck are you doing here?" said Lisa, covering herself up with the bed sheet.

"I live here. This is my flat." Robert replied, as he stood staring at the other person, who was now kneeling on the bed, and, he noticed, making no effort to cover herself up.

"You said you wouldn't be home until five twenty-seven. What time is it?" asked Lisa.

"Nearly three thirty. The game got postponed. It's all really foggy." Robert said, turning around and walking away from the bedroom as he attempted to collect his thoughts. The first thing he needed to address was why he was in total agreement with the voices in his head. The ones that were telling him that none of this could actually be perceived as gross misconduct and, under the circumstances, a written warning would probably suffice.

Saving Grace

Grace stood waiting outside the A & E ward at Homerton Hospital. Everywhere was quiet and dark at a quarter to five in the morning. Anybody with any sense would still be asleep on a freezing cold Wednesday morning in February, Grace assumed. She had just spent seven hours, most of it waiting, getting ten stitches put in a head wound and having various tests done before a doctor had finally allowed her to be discharged.

The hospital had been very good, though. She had to admit that. They'd even offered her a ride home in an ambulance. But, after convincing them that she was fine, and probably because she'd berated them for accusing her of being some old age pensioner who couldn't look after herself anymore, they'd agreed to let her call a mini cab from the reception area.

This must be it now, she thought, as a Vauxhall Cavalier pulled into the pick-up area.

"For a minute, I thought I was picking up Terry Butcher there," said the driver once Grace had sat down in the car.

"My name is Grace Meadows. Is this the right mini-cab or is it for somebody called Terry the butcher?"

"No, this is the right cab for Grace Meadows, but you look just like Terry Butcher with that bandage round your head."

"Who is this Terry Butcher? Is it a man or a woman? If it's a man, are you saying I look like a man?"

"No, no. Sorry, Lady. You know Terry Butcher, don't you? He's a footballer, plays for England. He helped England qualify for this year's World Cup in Italy by playing with a bandage on his head, just like yours."

"No, I don't like football. So, this footballer Terry Butcher, he's in Homerton hospital, is he? So, he's from round here then?"

"No, it's okay, forget it. This happened back in September last year."

"It must have been a bad accident if he's been in hospital all that time. Mine only happened last night, and they told me it was alright for me to go home now. I hope he doesn't have to wait too long for his mini cab. I bet he can't wait to get home now that they've finally let him out."

The cab driver drove in silence for a few minutes until they came to a stop at a red light. "How did you do it, then?" he asked.

"Oh, you know, I just fell over."

"What, you fell over for no reason, just like that? You been at the sherry?"

"I beg your pardon. No, I certainly haven't."

"You must have been having a good old go on the cheeba, then?" laughed the driver.

Grace decided to ignore the question as she had no idea what this man was talking about. It was all getting a bit too confusing after the night she'd had, and she just wanted to get home.

"I fell over once, as well," the cab driver, said, determined to make conversation to alleviate the boredom that was part and parcel of his job. "I stood up to get out of the bath, slipped, and went arse over tit. I had to go to the hospital, just like you. You can still see the scars."

"Oh dear, I'm sorry to hear that. Where are they?" Grace enquired.

"All down the wallpaper where I tried to stop myself falling," replied the driver.

Grace was now starting to regret turning down the Hospital's kind offer of an ambulance to take her home.

"Your house is a dangerous place," continued the cab driver. "I heard that ninety per cent of all accidents happen in your home. And more than half of all car accidents take place right near where you live."

While Grace would be one of the first to admit that the area had gone downhill over the years, she assumed that the cab driver wasn't referring to her house and decided not to confront him on this. It had been a long night and, for once, she didn't appreciate the opportunity to indulge in any kind of conversation with somebody.

She felt a sense of relief once she saw Hackney Downs, knowing that the mini cab would arrive at her house in a couple of minutes. She would have preferred a much quieter journey, but at least she wouldn't have the embarrassment of being seen getting out of an ambulance by one of her neighbours.

"Okay, thank you driver. Nice talking to you. You make sure you go back and get that Terry Butcher now. He must be really worried and think he's never going to get home."

* * *

Grace made herself a cup of tea and sat down. There was a pool of congealed blood on the kitchen floor that needed cleaning up. She'd fallen a few times recently but had never hurt herself before. Fortunately, although she'd banged her head this time and momentarily knocked herself out, she had regained consciousness after about twenty minutes. Following a considerable amount of effort, she was able to get herself up and standing again. It had taken quite a while for her to remember exactly what had happened. At first, she thought an intruder must have broken in and had hit her over the head. Then she called out for Harry, her husband, before remembering that he'd died just over four years ago. Grace had then stared at the telephone for a long time, trying to recall whether it was alright to phone her son. She decided against the idea as he'd moved out of London now, and it was probably too late to bother him. Grace finally convinced herself that she would have to go to the hospital but dismissed the idea of calling an ambulance. After cleaning herself up as best she could, Grace phoned for a cab and thankfully it was a different driver to the one she had just had, one who wasn't interested in talking or asking any questions.

Perhaps she shouldn't have lied to the nurse when she said she hadn't fallen over before, Grace wondered, but she didn't want to be forced to leave her house and go and live in an Old People's Home. She and Harry had worked hard to buy that house, had lived there for forty-five years, and now it was all theirs. Well, all Her's now that poor Harry had passed away. He was only sixty-six. Grace shuddered as it occurred to her that she was now older than Harry. What if she lived for another ten years? She'd be seventy-eight and Harry would still only be sixty-six. Would he still want to be with her when they met up again if she was twelve years older than him?

What on earth am I talking about? I must still be in shock, she decided. I really do miss Harry so much, though, and wish he was here now. He would look after me, I know he would. I hope that when I see him again, he still loves me as much as I still love him, even if I will be a lot older than he is. Maybe, wherever he is, he's already with someone else his own age and won't want to know me.

She started to cry and realized how silly she had been when she was a child, all those years ago, when she'd assumed that by the time a person reached the age she was now, they wouldn't have to cry ever again.

"Come on you need to snap out of it," she said out loud, before getting up and making her way to clean up the kitchen floor. "The sight of all that blood is obviously upsetting you."

While mopping up the blood, Grace tried to distract her mind from the gruesome task in hand by concentrating on something a little less unpleasant, like her only child, her son, Matthew. Maybe I could tell him what happened without him getting cross and shouting at me this time. Although I had better not, as when it happened, I wasn't wearing that newfangled panic alarm gadget he'd given me. The one he'd sent to me after I'd told him about the other falls. How old does he think I am? I bet he only got me one of those so I wouldn't disturb him if it happened again. I suppose it stops him having a guilty conscience for moving so far away. He was like a rat deserting a sinking ship when he got the chance to get out of Hackney, even though he'd lived here all his life. Now, all he keeps going on about is how much the area has improved and how much the houses are currently worth in this street. In fact, if I did have a nasty fall, I wouldn't be surprised if I pressed that alarm thing and it connected straight through to the estate agents, giving them the go ahead to put the house on the market right away. This last thought made Grace smile wryly, although she wasn't certain that it was actually making her feel any better.

Even by her standards, the rest of Wednesday and all-day Thursday were quiet and non-eventful. Grace was extra careful when she did have to get up and walk somewhere in the house.

She'd already decided that she wouldn't venture outside to the shops for a few days and would make do with whatever she had in the cupboard. February certainly wasn't getting any warmer and she'd be better off staying indoors. Also, however hard she tried to cover it up with one of her hats, Grace was convinced that her neighbours would still be able to notice that she was wearing a bandage. This was the last thing she wanted, especially if it made her look like a man or, worse still, a footballer.

* * *

At half past three on Friday afternoon, Grace was lying in a heap on her garden floor. She was finding it extremely difficult to get back up on to her feet again. Every time she tried, she had to give up because it was making her feel giddy. Her legs were numb, not just from the cold, and she had definitely done some serious damage to her wrist.

I'll just lie here for a little while longer and get my strength back, she thought. At least the neighbours can't see me like this. What would they say if they could see me lying on the floor like this in the middle of the afternoon? Oh, I feel so stupid. As hard as she tried, she couldn't come up with an excuse for how it had happened, and the only person she could direct any blame towards was Harry. "Oh, Harry this is all your fault. Why did you leave me all alone? I need you so much. I wish you were here with me now more than anything in the world."

The snow, which had been forecast, began to descend heavily. The clothes on the washing line, which Grace had intended to bring in before her fall, were starting to get wet. As she was contemplating another feeble attempt at getting herself up, she was distracted by a sound coming from her garden fence. Through blurred vision, Grace could just make out two men climbing over from the street into her back garden.

"Who's there?" said Grace. "Have you come to help me and take me to hospital?"

"Yes missus, that's right, we've come to save you," one of the men, said.

"Oh, thank goodness for that. I can't get up and I've hurt myself. I think I might need to see a doctor."

"Yeah, everything's going to be alright. We're the doctors, aren't we? My name is Dr Quincy and this Gentleman here is Dr 'Bones' McCoy," the other man said.

"Thank heavens you've come. I think I might have broken something," said Grace, relaxing a little now that help had arrived, and thinking it can't look too serious if both doctors were laughing.

The two men stepped over Grace's prostrate body and made their way into the house through the open back door. Once they were in the house the two men couldn't believe their luck.

"I thought we were going to have to smack that old bitch about a bit, but she's done it for us," said Quincy.

"Yeah, fucking doddle. Let's go and see what shit she's got that we can flog quickly and get the fuck out of here," said Bones. "What are we going to do about her afterwards, though?"

"Nothing, just leave her there."

"We can't do that. What if she dies? She's already got a bandage on her head. They'll think it was us and we'd be wanted for burglary and assault, and they might even try and do us for murder, as well."

"They're not going to catch us anyway, so it doesn't matter."

"Shouldn't we just call an ambulance once we've got what we want?"

"What the fuck's happened to you? Have you turned in to some sort of social worker, or something? You'll be doing meals on wheels and taking spastics to the seaside next. Anyway, there's fuck all here worth nicking. What a pile of shit. That television is older than me and there isn't even a fucking video recorder. The old bitch deserves to die. I'm not leaving here with nothing, though. What's in that chest of drawers?"

"A load of Dunn & Co clothes for some old man. I thought you said she lived here all on her own."

"Maybe he's upstairs hiding. Let's go up and see if he's there and if there's any jewelry worth taking. Then we can get the fuck out of this dump."

The two men were about to explore what treasures might lie upstairs when they heard a siren. After grabbing what they could, they ran back out into the garden, and clambered over the fence with an old radio and a pair of hardly worn (and in excellent condition) gentleman's beige slacks.

From her static position, Grace heard the men retreating. She assumed that they probably weren't the doctors she'd expected after all. Perhaps, that's the real doctors coming now. As far as she was aware, estate agents hadn't started using sirens just yet. The police will probably come later as well, she thought. What will the neighbours say? I bet the police will probably think I'm old and useless because I won't be able to describe either of those two men. But I'll show them I'm not. At least I can still remember their names, and, even if it's the last thing I do, I'm going to make sure I don't forget them.

Gran's Scheme of Things

Betty was relieved to be almost finished for the day at Woolworths in Dalston. She was starting to look forward to her evening when she noticed her daughter coming into the shop with Betty's grandson.

"What are you doing here?" said Betty.

"I need you to do me a favour," said her daughter.

When Betty didn't respond, Betty's daughter continued, "I need you to look after your grandson for me. Just for a couple of days. I'll come and get him at the weekend."

"Why? Where are you off to?"

"Nowhere. Look, I really need you to look after him for me. He is your grandson. I thought you liked looking after him."

"Tonight's my Bingo night," said Betty.

"Can't you miss Bingo for one week?"

"Oh, so you can go out and do whatever you want, but I can't. Is that it?" Betty said, now getting quite annoyed.

"I told you. I'm not going anywhere. I just need you to look after him for a couple of nights. It's really important. Anyway, isn't Harry at home to look after him?"

"He's on a late shift," replied Betty. "He won't be in until half nine. Anyway, what about tomorrow during the day, hasn't he got to go to school in the morning? It's my day off. Everybody knows I like a lie in on a Friday."

"No, he's on holiday. It's half term. You can take him to Clissold Park if you want. You know how much he likes it there."

"What, you want me to walk all the way up there with these feet?" Betty said.

"Look, you know I wouldn't ask you unless I really needed to. Can't you do it just this once?"

"You said that last time. I hope this isn't for the same reason again. If it is, I swear, I'll...."

"I'll wait with him outside until you get your coat," said Betty's daughter, turning around and walking with her son towards the shop's exit.

"Come on knucklehead," said Betty, taking her grandson's hand a little while later. "Let's get the bus, home."

"Can we go upstairs please, Gran?"

"No, we can't. What are you trying to do, kill me? I've been on me feet all day long. Me corns are jumping, and I haven't got the strength to go up a load of stairs as well. You'll be asking me to climb up Mount Everest next."

After the short bus journey, they were home in Betty's basement flat, which was in one of those roads very near to Stoke Newington Common.

"I can't wait to get these shoes off. These feet are really giving me gyp," said Betty, making herself comfortable on the settee and removing the offensive footwear. "That's better. Would you like something to eat? I can make you a sandwich, if you want. How about a nice slice of bread and dripping?"

"No thank you, Gran, I'm not very hungry. Mum said I shouldn't eat that anyway because I'll have a heart attack like Harry."

"What's she on about? When's the last time you saw a nine-year-old kid having a heart attack? Alright, how about a nice sugar sandwich instead?"

"No thanks. Mum said I shouldn't eat that as well, or I'll have false teeth like you and Harry."

"Bloody cheek! She doesn't know what she's talking about. How many nine-year-old kids do you know who have got false teeth?" Betty sat quietly, deep in thought, slowly shaking her head from left to right and occasionally tutting. After a short while she said, "I know, I've just remembered I've got a nice piece of tongue in the fridge. How about that in a sandwich? Though I suppose that mother of yours would still find something to complain about if you told her that I tried to give you one of them as well."

"Can I put Top of the Pops on please, Gran?"

"Of course you can."

A wave of sadness came over Betty as she thought about the relationship she had with her daughter, or rather, didn't have. Betty had tried to explain to her how hard things had been when she was younger, and why she didn't have much choice when she did what she had to do. She didn't have time to look after a young child, and there was a war going on, as well, which didn't exactly help. It didn't look like her daughter would ever truly understand though, and it certainly didn't look like she was ever going to forgive Betty, either.

Betty's thoughts were interrupted by the sound of the doorbell ringing, and she got up with an exaggerated sigh to go and open the door.

"Oh, Beryl, it's you, is it?" said Betty, letting in an older woman who looked all dressed up for a night out.

"Hello Betty, before I forget, I must ask you, how's that friend of yours, Elsie?"

"Oh, her. She dropped down dead over a year ago. I told you, I'm sure I did. What makes you ask about her?"

"I made myself toad in the hole for my dinner tonight and while I was eating it, it I suddenly made me think of your friend Elsie."

"What the bloody hell has toad in the hole got to do with Elsie?"

"I remembered that you once said that she liked a bit of toad in the hole, that's all. So, she passed away, then?"

"Yes! That's what I just said, she fell off her perch. I suppose we've all got to go sometime, whether we like it or not."

"Sorry," said Beryl. "I don't think you did tell me or, if you did, maybe I forgot." Then, quickly changing the subject, said "Are you all ready for Bingo, then? I'm feeling lucky tonight."

"No, I can't Beryl. I've got my grandson here."

"What, your daughter's boy?"

"Yes, that's what I said. My grandson."

"How come?" asked Beryl.

"His mother brought him in to the shop"

"What, your daughter?"

"Yes, that's what I said. His mother."

"What for?"

"So, I can look after him."

"Why?" asked Beryl.

"Fuck me, Beryl. You don't half ask a lot of questions. I don't know, do I?"

"It's Thursday. Bingo night. We always go to Bingo on Thursday," said Beryl, carefully structuring her words.

"Well, not tonight we're not. I've got to look after the boy. Anyway, I can't afford to go, I've spent all me happy money for the week. I ain't even got sixpence to scratch me arse with."

"Can't you borrow some off of Harry?" said Beryl, realizing too late what she had just done.

"He's not in until later."

"Well, I can lend you some. Would you..." Beryl said, deciding not to finish what she had intended to say.

"Would I what?" asked Betty

"If you would like me to lend you some, I will. You can pay me back out of your winnings. I feel really lucky tonight. I think the jackpot has got our names on it this week," said Beryl, who then started singing 'We're in the Money,' the song made famous by Ginger Rogers some forty years ago, when Beryl had the whole of the rest of her life to look forward to.

"Beryl, can you shut your bloody cake hole? The boy's trying to watch his Top of the Pops."

After staying silent for a couple of minutes, Beryl turned towards the young boy and said, "Do you like Top of the Pops, then?"

"Of course he fucking likes it. He wouldn't be watching it if he didn't, would he?" said Betty.

"Who's your favourite pop star then?" asked Beryl.

"Marc Bolan," said the boy, without taking his eyes away from the television screen.

"What do you like about him?" said Beryl.

"For fuck's sake Beryl! Can't you just leave him alone? He's trying to watch his Top of the Pops and all he can hear is you asking him a load of stupid bloody questions. What is it with you and all these questions tonight? Have you been watching that University fucking Challenge, or something?"

"Someone's got the right hump, haven't they?" replied Beryl

"Well, I've been on me feet all day at work, knocking me pipe out. Not sitting on me arse watching University Challenge and eating toad in the fucking hole, like some people round here I could mention."

"Sounds like you could do with a good night out. Bingo is just what the doctor ordered for an old, grumpy chops like you."

"Fuck off. I ain't fucking grumpy. And I ain't fucking old, either. You're no spring chicken yourself, you cheeky cow." Betty exclaimed as she walked out of the room.

Betty appeared a while later, wearing much smarter clothes and having applied a noticeable amount of make-up.

"Have you changed your mind, then?" said Beryl, smiling.

"What does it look like? I could do with a good night out. I'm off tomorrow and I don't want to miss my Bingo. Harry will be home at half nine. That means the boy will only be on his own for a couple of hours. He'll be alright here just watching the telly. He's a sensible boy, let me just have a quick word with him. I'm feeling lucky tonight as well."

* * *

Betty returned a little after 10 o'clock, later that night, to find Harry sitting in his armchair watching the television.

"What are you watching?" said Betty.

"Telly," answered Harry.

"Ha bloody ha. Very funny," Betty said. "I'll save that one for when they put me in an old people's home, then I'll piss myself. I mean what are you watching?"

"I'm watching Telly. The bloke's name is Telly Savalas," said Harry, chuckling at his own joke.

"Who's he when he's at home, then?"

"Kojak."

"He's got even less hair than you," said Betty. "How comes he ain't got any hair, is he supposed to be sick?"

"No, he's a detective."

"Who's he after, then?"

"Some gang in New York who've taken over a geriatric hospice and are holding all the patients hostage in the basement. They've demanded a million dollars and a helicopter to escape, otherwise they're going to start shooting the hostages one by one every fifteen minutes."

"Where's the boy, asleep?" said Betty, having now lost all interest in Kojak.

"What boy?"

"Stop acting the goat, Harry. I'm not in the mood for it tonight. You know. My grandson."

"How am I supposed to know?"

"I left him here. Wasn't he here when you came home?"

"No. What, you left him here, all on his own?"

"It was only for a couple of hours. You know full well it's Bingo night. Me and Beryl went, we had to, we were both feeling lucky. Complete waste of time that was, we won absolutely fuck all. Maybe he went to bed early. I'll have a look in the spare bedroom."

Betty returned a few minutes later with the news that Harry was dreading. "No, I can't find him anywhere. He's not in the spare room or in our bedroom. I've even looked in the toilet."

"Well, where is he, then?" Harry said, getting up and switching off the television. Kojak's dilemma no longer seemed important now that Harry had his own detective work to do. For a split second he wished that Kojak was with them both right now. At least Kojak would have some idea about what to do next.

Betty, having now realized the seriousness of the situation, began to cry.

"Look, he can't have gone very far, we'll find him," said Harry, looking around the living room for any clues, however unimportant they might at first seem.

"Well, he's definitely not here," Harry said, just to give himself time to think. "We should call the police."

"We can't do that. They'll do me for going to Bingo and leaving him here all on his own. It's all your fault, anyway. None of this would have happened if you'd got home earlier."

"I told you I wasn't coming home from work until half nine."

"You come home late and even though my grandson's gone missing, all you can do is put the telly on and sit on your fat arse watching some bloke who's got something wrong with him called Kodak, or whatever his fucking name is, trying to save a load of old fucking coffin dodgers."

"Betty, calm down. I'm calling the police. They'll know what to do."

* * *

After what seemed like an agonizingly long period of time to Betty and Harry, but was in reality just under an hour, the doorbell rang. Betty quickly went and answered the door.

"Mrs. Jackson?" said a policeman standing on the doorstep.

"Yes, come in," said Betty

"I'm PC Thomas and this lovely young lady here is Miss Taylor. Sorry, I should say WPC Taylor. We're from Stoke Newington

Police Station. You called us about a child who's supposedly gone missing."

"Yes, that's my grandson."

"And this gentleman here I presume is Mr. Jackson, the boy's grandfather?"

"No, sorry, I'm not the boy's real grandfather," said Harry. "But I am Mr. Jackson, Mrs. Jackson's husband."

"I see," said PC Thomas, writing something down in his notebook. "And when exactly did you last see the boy, Mr. Jackson?"

"About two weeks ago," said Harry. "His mum brought him round for the weekend."

"What? "He's been missing for two weeks, and you've only just decided report it," said PC Thomas.

"No," said Betty. "Don't listen to him. He got home too late tonight to look after him, and by the time I came home, he said the boy had already disappeared."

"I see," said PC Thomas, who wrote something else down in his notebook. "So, when was the last time either of you saw him?"

"About seven thirty, when he was watching Top of the Pops," said Betty.

"And then he suddenly disappeared?" said PC Thomas.

"No, that's when I went out," Betty said, looking down at the beige circular patterns woven into her brown and red carpet.

"How long were you out for?"

"Only until about ten"

"So, you left him, watching Top of the Pops, for two and a half hours. Was anybody else here?"

"I don't think it's on for that long. I think it might only be on for half an hour and that's more than enough, I can tell you. I don't think anybody could stomach it for two and a half hours.

There would have been something else on afterwards, though. I'm not sure exactly what. I can take a look in the Radio Times if you really want me to. What I do know is that Harry said he came home at nine thirty for his Kodak," said Betty

"I see," said PC Thomas, once again writing something in his notebook. When he had finished, he continued. "This a hobby of yours, is it sir? Pictures. Looking at–"

"No. It's not on at the pictures," Betty interjected. "You know what I'm talking about. He isn't very well. He's got that disease. That's why all his hair's fallen out. It happened to this woman I worked with, as well. She got it. Dorothy Johnstone was her name. With an 'e' on the end if you want to write it down. She was a strange woman. Always wore clothes that didn't suit her. Before she got ill, everybody used to say she looked just like mutton dressed as lamb, but after all her hair fell out, she started dressing more appropriately. So, if you ask me, I reckon it was probably a blessing in disguise."

"I think I'd better speak to Mr. Jackson alone," said PC Thomas. "I tell you what Mrs. Jackson, why don't you and young Jenny here, sorry, WPC Taylor, go into the kitchen and make us all a nice cup of tea. WPC Taylor knows how I like it, don't you, love?"

PC Thomas looked over at Harry and winked but received no response from Harry. Harry had already decided that he had taken an instant dislike to this man and wished the Police station had sent somebody different. This policeman was nothing like Kojak. Neither in his appearance nor in his professional manner.

PC Thomas looked slowly around the living room. He then wrote something else down in his notebook. "I think we ought to start from the beginning. How old is your grand…? Sorry, I should say step grandson?"

"He's only nine. I'll show you a picture of him if that'll help. It's quite a recent one." Harry went over and picked up a framed photograph they kept on top of the television set and passed it over to the policeman. The picture appeared to be taken in a park and showed a small boy smiling broadly at the camera. He was wearing a yellow, Arsenal 1971 FA Cup Final shirt, which looked like it had been washed numerous times over the past couple of years.

"Did you take this picture with that Kodak of yours? I see he likes his football," said PC Thomas. "Is he interested in anything else?"

"He likes his pop music, as well. Especially that group, T.Rex. He once said to me 'I wish I came from outer space like Marc Bolan does.' I didn't have the heart to tell him that the bloke used to live just down the road from here. No, he's a great kid. A bit quiet and a little bit shy, perhaps, but he's a really lovely boy."

"So, he's like a real grandson to you, would you say?"

"I suppose so, yes."

"But he's not your real grandson, is he?"

"No, but I've known him since he was born. I'd do absolutely anything for him. He means the world to me."

Harry had mixed feelings about seeing Betty and the policewoman return with a tray of tea and biscuits. While he was pleased to no longer be alone with this policeman, he didn't want either of the women to notice the tears that had formed in his eyes.

"What about his parents, have you told them he's missing?" asked PC Thomas, reaching for his cup of tea and helping himself to a few of the biscuits on offer.

"No, not yet. We didn't know what to do, or what to say to them, so we called you first," replied Betty.

"Don't you think you should give them a call? They've got a right to know that their son has vanished. I would have thought they would have been the first people you would have contacted," PC Thomas said.

"Well, we've never really got on that well," said Betty. "We disagree on a number of things. A lot more than just sandwiches, if the truth be known."

"Well, this might bring you closer together. Give them a call. They might be able to give us a clue as to where the little lad might have got to," said PC Thomas.

"Alright then, if you think that it'll help. Go on Harry, give them a call," said Betty.

"Me? It's your daughter."

"But you're a lot better at using the phone than I am," Betty replied.

Just as Harry was slowly getting up to make his way over to the telephone stand, everybody was suddenly aware of another presence in the room.

"Why are the police here, Gran?"

"Oh, thank fuck for that. Where in hell have you been?" Betty said.

"I was hiding in the wardrobe."

"What the bloody hell were you doing hiding in the wardrobe? You silly nincompoop. You frightened the life out of us."

"I wanted to give Harry a surprise when he came home, but I fell asleep."

"A surprise? You would have given him another bloody heart attack. Come here," said Betty, as she held her arms wide open in order to give her grandson the hug, she had at one point feared she would never be able to do again.

"Ouch! That hurt me."

"Sorry, did I hug you too hard? I'm just so pleased to see you," Betty said, smiling for the first time that day.

"My back is sore and it really hurt."

"Well, you shouldn't sleep in the wardrobe should you then, you daft ninny," said Betty, this time laughing for the first time that day.

"Would it be alright if we just have a little look, please?" said WPC Taylor to the boy, determined to prove that she hadn't just been brought along for tea making duties.

The boy turned away from everybody and lifted his t-shirt, in order to show his back which was covered in welts and bruises.

"They do look sore, don't they. Do you know how you got those marks on your back?" said WPC Taylor.

"I was naughty."

"What did you do?" WPC Taylor asked. "It's alright, you can tell us."

"If I tell you, I won't get arrested, will I?" said the boy turning round to face the policewoman.

"No, I promise you won't," WPC Taylor replied. "Cross my heart."

"My mum said I was playing her up and getting on her nerves."

"So did your mum give you those marks, then?" enquired WPC Taylor.

"No. She told my dad when he came home from work last night. It was really late and he was angry. You won't put him in prison, will you? My mum will be upset if you do. Then he'll be cross and hit me again when they let him out."

"No, don't worry. We won't put him in prison. We might just talk to him though, and ask him not to hurt you anymore," WPC

Taylor said. "Is that what made you fall asleep in the wardrobe? Was it because you were very tired after what happened last night?"

"Maybe. I don't know." The boy replied. His voice barely audible even in the silent living room.

"That's alright. If you can try and remember everything that happened, and you don't mind telling us, we can make sure that it won't happen to you anymore," said WPC Taylor, kneeling down to face the young boy.

"My mum sent me to bed early, but I couldn't sleep because I knew my dad was going to hit me when he came home. I heard him open the front door and my mum told him that I'd been naughty. Then I could hear him coming up the stairs to my room, and he pulled me out of bed, and he kicked me and hit me lots of times with the big stick that he keeps up on the wall to warn me not to do bad things, and I couldn't sleep afterwards because it really hurt and I was crying. Then I was scared because he said I mustn't move or say anything and if I did, he would hit me again. Then I was worried he would be really cross and hit me because I had wet the bed."

When the boy finished, he was so surprised to see both his Gran and Harry crying, that this made him cry as well. Even the policeman looked a little bit unsettled and continued to remain unusually quiet.

"Hey, come on, don't cry. And don't worry. Nobody's going to hurt you ever again," said WPC Taylor, hoping that it would be a very long time before the boy realized that she had lied to him just to make him feel better. "Are you going to be alright here with your Grandparents tonight?" WPC Taylor added.

"Yes, I like it here," the boy answered, trying to control his sobbing.

"You know what? I'll tell you something for nothing. This really fucking boils my piss." said Betty, after she had composed herself. "People shouldn't have kids if they're not prepared to look after them properly. Everyone knows I'd do anything for that boy."

"Can we go to Clissold Park tomorrow, please Gran?"

"Of course, we can, sweetheart. Whatever you want," replied Betty, not giving her feet a moment's consideration for the first time that day.

Not A Prostitute You Know

Mike was now feeling drunk enough not to want to go home. He'd long gone past caring that he hadn't told Rachel he was going to be back later than expected. Surely, Rachel would have already guessed by now that he was in it for the long haul, he convinced himself, even though he had assured her that morning that he wouldn't be back late. It wasn't like they had any plans for the evening anyhow, and he seldom went out straight from work on a Friday anymore, not since he had moved into Rachel's flat six months ago.

A colleague in his department at the Insurance Company was leaving to have a baby, and as she was one of the few people he worked with that he quite liked talking to, he decided he would show his face and have a couple of drinks to say goodbye to her.

Nearly everybody, including the heavily pregnant host, who had started off the evening in the reserved space at the Vino Veritas Wine Bar on Cannon Street, in the heart of the City of London, had left by now. And the last person there, other than himself, was Anita, a personal secretary to one of the Company Directors. He had very rarely spoken to Anita before and the impression he had of her was that she always seemed quite aloof.

Anita was probably even more drunk than Mike and was starting to show all the effects of somebody who had been drinking solidly for four and a half hours without having had a substantial meal beforehand.

"It's so good that you came out tonight, Mike. You never come out with us on a Friday anymore."

"I usually have better things to do."

"But you're having a good time tonight, I hope."

"Yeah, it's been great."

"You're not going yet, are you?"

"Why, what have you got in mind?"

"Let's have another drink and discuss it," said Anita, struggling to stay seated on her bar stool and get her purse out of her handbag at the same time.

"Will you go and get them, please Mike? The last time I went the guy behind the bar asked me if I was alright and suggested that I might have already had too much to drink."

Mike returned a little while later with another bottle of house white wine.

"I wasn't sure he was going to serve me, either," said Mike. "He asked me if I was with you and was I absolutely sure that you were okay."

"What did you say?"

"I said you were fine and that you were in perfectly capable hands, anyway," replied Mike.

"Aw! You're so nice. I'm so glad you came out tonight. I really like being here with you. Will you really look after me?"

"Of course," said Mike, wondering where this could all be heading. While filling both of their glasses, he took a closer look at Anita and realized she was much more attractive than he had previously noticed. He decided that he was prepared to look after her and would personally accompany her home to ensure her absolute safety. "We will need to go soon. I think the place is closing up," Mike added.

"But it's only about eight. The night is still young," Anita declared, theatrically waving her arms about and causing her bar stool to wobble considerably.

"It's actually twenty past ten," Mike said looking at his watch. "I think this place usually closes around now. Are you going to be alright getting home by yourself?"

"I'm not drunk, you know. Why does everybody keep thinking I'm drunk?" Anita replied, as she adjusted her precarious position on the bar stool, knocking over her wine glass in the process, and only just saving herself from falling by grabbing hold of Mike's thigh.

"I know you're not drunk," said Mike. "I just wondered if you would be okay going home, or do you want somebody to come back with you to make sure you get home safely?"

"Who have you got in mind, the barman?" Anita laughed loudly, softening her grip on Mike's thigh but keeping her hand in the same place.

"No, I'll come back with you to make sure you get home alright. If that's okay with you and you want me to, of course."

"You don't know where I live," said Anita, surprisingly introducing some rationality into the conversation.

"I assumed it wouldn't be that far away. Where exactly do you live, then?" enquired Mike

"Hither Green."

"Where on earth is that?"

"It's close. Only one stop on the train from London Bridge."

"Really? I've never heard of it."

"Well, you have now. So, now you know where I live, do you still want to take me home?"

"Of course. If you'd still like me to."

Anita took another drink from her refilled glass and looked blankly at Mike. "Do you fancy me?"

Although Mike was well aware that this was the direction the conversation was heading, the directness of Anita's question momentarily threw him off guard, and he did not reply immediately.

"Well? Be honest. You do, don't you?" enquired Anita again, this time expecting a much swifter response to her perfectly reasonable question.

"Yes, I do. I think you're really sexy," Mike finally replied, deciding now to get the ball rolling.

"Do you want to sleep with me? asked Anita.

"Yes," replied Mike.

"How much would you pay me to sleep with you?" Anita said, with a peculiar look on her face.

This, Mike thought, was probably more of an unreasonable question than the previous one. Assuming Anita was only joking, he decided to continue flirting, and even made himself cringe by saying, "Who said anything about sleeping?"

"Alright. How much - would you pay - to spend the night - with me?" Anita slowly whispered into Mike's ear.

Mike, deciding to go along with the charade which, he had to confess he was now finding quite stimulating, even if it was all becoming a lot more confusing than he'd originally expected, slowly whispered back, "How much - do you charge - for a fuck?"

"I'm not a prostitute, you know," screamed Anita, as she attempted to get off of her bar stool in one movement, which she should have realized by now, in her current state, was impossible.

"I'm really sorry," said Mike, as he helped Anita up from the floor. "I thought it was a game."

"What? You think calling me a prostitute is a game?" said Anita, frantically dusting herself down.

"I didn't mean that, honestly."

"You wait until I tell everybody at work you called me a prostitute and offered me money to have sex with you."

"I didn't. This has all been a big misunderstanding, and I'm really sorry if I've offended you in any way at all."

"What? Are you telling me you that you wouldn't be offended if someone called you a prostitute? And then offered you money to have sex with them. Who do you think you are, anyway, God's gift to women? I wouldn't sleep with you if you paid me."

At this point the previously suspicious barman came towards them with a smug 'I told you so' look on his face and suggested that perhaps it wouldn't be such a bad idea if they both decided to vacate the premises immediately.

* * *

Mike decided he had better wait for Anita, if only to try and sort out the confusion which had arisen and put the record straight. As soon as they both stepped outside into the cold night air, Anita collapsed.

"Should I get you a cab?" asked Mike, helping Anita back on to her feet not for the first time that evening.

"Why, do you think I'm drunk as well as being a prostitute? Well, I'm not either of those things. I don't need a cab; it was just the fresh air that made me fall over. Why would I get a cab at only half past eight in the evening when I can still get a train? You can take me to London Bridge station if I can trust you to keep your hands to yourself."

"Of course, though its actually just gone ten thirty," said Mike, steadying Anita and helping her to walk in the direction they needed to go. "It's quite a way over the bridge," continued Mike. "Are you sure we shouldn't get a cab?"

"We?" said Anita a little more loudly than was necessary. "Do you think you're coming back with me after everything you said about me? And still expect to pay me to sleep with you?"

"No. I meant just to the train station," Mike answered, now wishing he could just leave Anita to make her own way there. Or better still, that it was only five thirty on Friday and he had gone straight home and none of this was actually happening.

"You'll have to hold my hand to help me," said Anita. "I really don't know why you've made me walk all this way."

They walked over London Bridge in silence. Mike decided that now was probably not a good time to discuss the matter. Hopefully, Anita would have forgotten everything by the morning and nothing of this would ever be mentioned again. They might even laugh about this one day. No, that wouldn't happen, Mike corrected himself. Either the whole episode would never be spoken of, or Anita would tell at least one person in the office everything that she thought had happened. Word would soon get round that not only did he try and get her to sleep with him, he was prepared to pay her good money in order to do so. Although, as he recalled, no fixed price had ever been established.

The weekend was ruined already, and it was still only Friday.

Anita put her arm around Mike's waist to steady herself as she struggled further to walk. "Put your arm around me, Mike."

"Okay, we're almost there now," said Mike, noticing the relief in his voice.

"Will you wait with me until my train arrives, Mike?"

"Of course, I will," Mike replied. Now thinking that if he did everything Anita wanted him to, there might still be a good chance she would forgive him for what had happened, and not mention any of this to their colleagues.

They eventually found the correct platform and managed to work out that the next train to Hither Green would be arriving in ten minutes.

"Will you put both your arms around me Mike? I'm cold?"

"Sure. The train will be here very soon though."

"Will you kiss me while we wait for the train? I am wearing underwear from Agent Provocateur."

Before Mike even had a chance to consider whether or not this would be a good idea, or perhaps something he would admit to wanting to do, both he and Anita were kissing each other passionately, albeit drunkenly.

"I'm so glad you fancy me, Mike. But I'm still very cross that you suggested paying me money to go to bed with you. You never did tell me how much were you going to pay me, did you?"

The train promptly pulled into the platform. Anita looked at Mike expectantly, but, at that present moment in time, Mike was giving nothing away.

* * *

"Just here is fine," Mike said to the taxi driver as they drove along Green Lanes later that night, and the cab pulled over at one of the roads opposite Clissold Park.

"Are you sure here's alright?" said the taxi driver.

"Yes, it's perfect. I'm just over the other side of the barrier up the road," Mike lied. "So, you can't drive through there anyway."

"If you'd told me where you were going before, I would have gone a different way round to avoid the barrier."

"It's alright, I don't mind walking the rest of the way. I could probably do with clearing my head a bit before going home."

"Like that is it?" laughed the taxi driver. "The missus gonna have your bollocks for yo-yos, is she? Good luck, mate. I'm glad I'm not in your shoes. Let me give you a piece of advice. Next time you'd be better off telling the driver exactly where you want to go, and he can go the right way for you. Avoid the barrier. Save you walking."

"Look. It doesn't matter. It's my fault. Here is good, honestly."

"Okay, but I still wish you'd told me where you wanted to go when you got in, I could have gone the other way round. It's a lot easier for me to get another fare round the other side. Have a bit of consideration for others next time, eh?"

Mike paid the driver and got out of the taxi. He waited until the cab had driven off and began the walk back to Rachel's flat to receive, no doubt, a frosty reception. Everywhere was deathly quiet and it therefore came as something of a surprise when he heard a woman's voice shouting behind him.

"Stop! Stop! Please! Stop!"

Mike turned around and saw a young woman running towards him. Before he had the chance to decide whether to stop or ignore her, the woman had caught up with him. By now he could tell that she was clearly in a distressed state.

"Help me? I'm in danger," said the woman.

"Who from, and what do you want me to do?" Mike said in as much of a sympathetic a tone as he could manage.

"My name's Sarah and I'm homeless and if I don't find somewhere to stay tonight, I'm in real danger."

A quick evaluation by Mike revealed that the woman did look genuinely scared. She was relatively clean and appeared to be crying actual tears. "I'm not sure what I can do," he said. "I would suggest that you come and stay with us, at my girlfriend's place, but I'm not sure that would be a good idea tonight."

"Can you give me some money for a shelter?" Sarah pleaded.

"I haven't got any cash on me," said Mike.

"There's an ATM back there, at Sainsburys," said Sarah.

Sarah continued to cry realistic tears and decided that she would have to elaborate in order to substantiate her case. "I'm homeless but I'm not a prostitute, you know. Everybody thinks I'm a prostitute, but I'm not. Even though I haven't got any teeth. Somebody's after me and If I don't find somewhere to stay tonight..."

"Alright, I'll see what I can do. How much do you need for the shelter?"

"Twenty pounds."

"Really?"

"Yes, honestly. Thank you so much. I really appreciate it."

"Look, I really do want to help you if you are in danger, but you've got to promise me you will definitely go and stay in a shelter. If I give you twenty pounds, how do I know you won't go and spend it all on drink and drugs?" enquired Mike.

"I wouldn't do that."

"I would," said Mike, trying to cheer Sarah up. Sarah continued to cry though, and Mike walked with her back to the ATM, still not fully sure he was doing the right thing but, he thought, under the circumstances what else could he possibly do?

* * *

Mike opened the front door as quietly as he possibly could, hoping that Rachel was asleep.

"Where the fuck have you been? And what fucking time do you call this?" screamed Rachel, as soon as Mike was in the flat. "Do you know I've been waiting up all fucking night for you? Why didn't you fucking phone me?" Rachel continued.

Mike had expected Rachel to be angry, though perhaps he had underestimated how much. Not knowing which question to answer first, Mike just said, "Sorry."

"Sorry? Sorry? You waltz in here at two o'clock in the morning and all you've got to say for yourself is fucking 'Sorry'!"

Although Mike felt strangely compelled to tell Rachel everything that had happened, he had to decide how much of the truth he was prepared to divulge. He had never heard Rachel swear so much and knew he had to be careful with his explanation. "Can we talk about this another time? I've had a really weird night and I'm tired. I'll tell you all about it in the morning."

"No chance, Buster! You're going to give me a full explanation as to where you've been all night, and why you didn't even bother to tell me you weren't coming home."

"I'm really sorry if I worried you."

"I'm not worried, I'm fucking fuming."

"I can tell."

"So, where were you all this time?"

"Like I told you this morning. I went to someone's leaving drink after work."

"Until now?"

"I would have been home sooner, but I needed to give a prostitute twenty pounds."

"What?" screamed Rachel, as she began to pace backwards and forwards across the living room floor.

"Well, she might not have actually been a prostitute. It was all a bit confusing. But she did ask me to give her money."

"Why the fuck did you go and give her twenty pounds?"

"I think she desperately needed it. I thought it would help. I hoped it would make her feel better."

"You idiot. She definitely saw you coming."

"No, she didn't. What was I supposed to do? She approached me. She kept asking me to stop. She wasn't really making much sense by the end and seemed genuinely frightened, and she was sobbing. I wasn't sure if I could really trust her, but I gave her twenty pounds and that was it, honestly. I don't know, it just felt like it was the right thing to do."

* * *

On Sunday, Mike awoke on the sofa for the second morning running. Rachel was clearly still annoyed and wasn't yet speaking to him normally, but at least the effing and jeffing had gradually ceased. He made them both a cup of coffee and took these in to the bedroom, knocking softly before entering the room.

"Is it alright if I come in? I've made you a nice cup of coffee."

Rachel who was sitting up in bed, ignored him and gave the impression that she was engrossed in looking at The Guardian website on her tablet.

"Just to let you know, I've transferred the money towards your mortgage for this month into your bank account," Mike said, again to another blank response. "Is it alright if I get into bed with you?"

Rachel suddenly turned towards Mike and said, "Oh, so because you've paid me some money that we've both agreed is owed to me, you think that makes it alright for you to get into bed with me now, do you? I'm not one of your prostitutes, you know."

"Oh, come on Rachel, you know I didn't mean that. How long is this going to go on for? I really am so sorry about everything that happened on Friday and promise nothing like that will ever happen again. I had too much to drink and shouldn't have carried on without letting you know, but the battery on my phone was dead, and I wasn't thinking rationally. You know how it is. Look, the weekend is nearly over already. Can't we have a nice Sunday together? I just know I've got a bad week coming up and really want to make the most of today."

"I'm getting up now. I want some breakfast," said Rachel

"I'll make it for you," said Mike, making his way to the kitchen, hoping he was slowly on course to restoring Rachel's trust in him.

Mike went about selecting food from the fridge and opening and closing cupboards and drawers, taking out the utensils and crockery required to prepare a breakfast Rachel would never forget. Rachel sat at the breakfast bar and continued looking at her tablet while Mike began the cooking. After a short while Rachel looked up at Mike and said, "Where in hell is Hither Green?"

"Absolutely no idea. Why do you ask?" Mike replied, without turning round to face Rachel.

"There's a horrible story in the news about some woman who was strangled to death in her own home. It happened in the early hours of Saturday morning; or so the police think. They reckon she must have known the killer as there was no sign of any forced entry."

Mike continued to prepare breakfast, relieved that Rachel was back on his side and talking to him again. "That sounds terrible. What else does it say?"

"Nothing, that's about it. Except that the police are still working on trying to piece everything together."

"Of course," said Mike. He carried on cooking and smirked as he wondered what the detective investigating the murder would have thought of the twenty-pound note discovered on the victim's naked body.

Time Wasted

He knew it was going to be a bad day but hadn't imagined it would be this bad. At least the train journey home at this time in the afternoon would be quiet, he thought, trying to find at least one thing positive to prove that not everything that was happening that day would end up being disastrous.

The train was already in the platform at Liverpool Street station although, to his disappointment, it wasn't due to leave for another nine minutes. As he boarded, he chose one of the many empty seats in the final carriage. This wasn't part of any strategic plan that would make his exit at Rectory Road station any easier, but more to do with the way he was feeling. His body was telling him that it couldn't manage to walk any further along the platform, it needed to sit down soon. Even then, he knew that this wouldn't completely cure his pounding headache and the nauseous feeling inside his stomach. From experience, he fully appreciated that this condition would not leave him alone until tomorrow at the very earliest. You had to take it one easy step at a time and sitting down at the earliest opportunity was the first stage to recovery. Step 2 would be to try and eat something when he got home. Step 3, drink lots of tomato juice. Step 4, take another couple of pain killers and sleeping tablets. This would then enable the final procedure, Step 5, get a good night's sleep.

He would wake up the next morning feeling no worse than usual and ready to face the day. Except, tomorrow, he already knew, would be completely different. For a start, even though it was Wednesday, he wouldn't be required to go into work. There is nothing unnatural about this when a company you work for decides to instantly dismiss you. He was in no fit state to address this problem now, though. He needed to prioritise and, right now, getting home and starting his recuperation was paramount.

For something to do, he leaned forward and looked along the walk-through carriages all the way to the front of the train but had to stop when this started to make him feel giddy. The phrase 'commuter friendly train' came into his head. This had been used to describe this style of train when it was first introduced, and all it really meant was that you had a better chance of getting on the thing in the morning. It certainly didn't seem to have the effect of making the commuters any friendlier. At least he wouldn't have to put up with that again for a little while. Another positive to add to the ever-growing list.

There were only a few other people on the train. Maybe they had all been sacked as well, he thought. This made him feel better for a few seconds, but then he went back to feeling sorry for himself again. Perhaps if he could think of someone else who's fault this all was, it might help. Though, as much as he tried, he hated to admit that he probably only had himself to blame.

* * *

Maybe Charlie should take some responsibility for this. After all, he was the one who suggested meeting up at five-thirty last night. That usually meant that he wanted to go and see his girlfriend, and once they had completed the deal, they would only have time for a couple of pints together. Why didn't he say he'd split up with his girlfriend and wasn't doing anything later that evening? It's alright for him, he doesn't have to get up for work the next morning. Also, it was Charlie who'd suggested that they both carry on after the pub had shut and had got out the bottle of quality bourbon once they'd finished all the beers they'd brought in with them. It was Charlie who brought out the coke to go with it as well. Not the usual imitation coke, either. No, we are talking about the coke that might actually have some cocaine in it.

At four-thirty in the morning they had finally called it a day. Five seconds to do the transaction, eleven hours to celebrate it being completed successfully. It was good to know Charlie, even if he did lead you astray and cause you to lose your job. At least he was someone you could trust when you bought coke. As he invariably said, whenever he sold him a few grammes, 'This is quality gear and not to be sniffed at'. He also knocked a few quid off as well, now that they had become good mates, which gave you peace of mind that you weren't paying through the nose for it.

He had no idea how long it had taken him to walk home. It normally only took about fifteen minutes, but when you're walking like a penguin, it's possible that it might have taken longer. The next thing he remembered is being woken up by a continuous horrible groaning sound. It took quite a while before he realized that this noise was actually coming from him. A cry for help, totally in vain, but one which he persisted with for some considerable time, just in case he was wrong about there being absolutely nobody around who was likely to come to his aid.

After finally conceding defeat and facing the harsh reality that a pretty, kindly, young nurse was not about to respond to his cries, he forced himself to get up. Recognizing at once that he could barely stand up straight, he fell backwards into the safe haven of his warm bed. He was sure the alarm had already gone off, it certainly felt later than seven-thirty, but dreaded looking to see what the actual time was. After plucking up the courage, he slowly raised his left arm and squinted at his watch but could only make out one hand showing on the face. Did he somehow break his watch last night? The one that Jenny had bought him for his thirtieth birthday last year. There was a feeling of relief followed by panic when it struck him that his watch was in perfect order and was in fact showing that it was ten minutes to ten.

    He continued to stay in the foetal position groaning loudly again, still not completely convinced that help would not arrive. His thoughts turned to Jenny, as they did most mornings shortly after he awoke, but she wasn't coming back. Even if she had been there, she wouldn't have shown him any sympathy and would have told him what she always did, 'That it serves you right for spending a fortune on something you put up your nose just to make you chat shit and act like a cunt.' That never failed to make him laugh, and while he had to admit that she was absolutely right, it didn't stop him from continuing to do it.

    After briefly considering phoning in sick, he dismissed the idea in order to prove a point to himself. He'd once read that as soon as you start taking time off work caused by alcohol or drug intake, it was the first stage to admitting that you had a drink or drug problem. There was also the course he was expected to attend at eleven–thirty that morning to consider. Some corporate bullshit called 'How to Be a High Performing Team Player' or something like that. He groaned out loud again. The HR woman at his company had already accused him of not taking these things seriously enough last week, when she summoned him to her office to find out why he'd responded to the invite for the 'How to Stop

Procrastinating In The Workplace' course by asking if it would be alright if he could do it another day.

* * *

At the risk of greater pain, he maneuvered his body in order to see the train indicator on the platform. There were still four minutes to go before the train left. A few more sacked people had now boarded and were probably also regretting getting out of bed that morning. If only he hadn't had to go on that ridiculous course, he could have got away with it and still have a job. He'd got through similar days before without any repercussions, even in those instances when he'd fallen asleep, mostly in the toilet, but once while sitting up at his desk. Why did he have to go on that course today of all days? Even so, why couldn't he have just kept his mouth shut for another few minutes?

* * *

He'd never heard such a bunch of bollocks. Surely, the bloke who was coming out with all this bullshit couldn't actually believe it, could he? When everybody arrived in the course room, the instructor was already waiting there in front of his whiteboard, with a big shit-eating grin on his face, as if he'd just come up with the best idea in the history of mankind. TOGETHER. EVERYONE. ACHIEVES. MORE. This was written in large black letters, with the first letter of each word circled by a red marker pen. The instructor then decided to waffle on for what seemed like an eternity. The clock on the wall must have been broken. It didn't appear to have moved whenever he looked at it, which was every time the instructor had his back to him. The instructor must have caught him doing this though, because he then started directing his questions at him. He could feel the relief from everybody else present in the room now that he'd been singled out for special attention, leaving them free to think about what they would have delivered by some desperate suicidal lunatic on a bike for their dinner that night, and who they were going to drag up from their memory archives in order to knock one out to before they went to sleep.

"So, which famous person said, 'There is no I in team, but there is in win'?" said the instructor, walking over and standing directly in front of him.

"No idea," he replied.

"Come on, it's low hanging fruit," the instructor said. "This is a famous quote we can all use to better ourselves in our day-to-day professional lives, and one which will help us achieve our performance goals and objectives."

"I really don't know," he tried to say as normally and politely as possible, although now fully aware of just how frighteningly croaky his voice sounded.

"Alright. You've reached out to me. So, let's synergize. I'll open the kimono and reveal some crucial information. We'll call it a good example of teamwork," said the instructor, smiling. "What if I said you'd be on the right lines if you think of the name, Jordan?"

"What, it was Peter Andre?"

"Are you taking the Mickey? It's Michael. Michael Jordan. Michael Jeffrey Jordan said it. The greatest basketball player in the history of basketball. I'd like you to stand up and say this important phrase in front of everybody here, please. Repeat after me. There is no I in team, but there is in win."

"No. I don't want to."

"Why not? Say it now, out loud, with me," said the instructor clicking his fingers. "There is no I in team but there is in win."

"No, you've already said it enough times, I think we get the idea now."

"Let this be a valuable lesson to everybody else here," the instructor said. "I'm sure that, along with your visualizations about getting on all fours and leveraging full impact from a drill down, you've also given a lot of consideration to what you would say have been your top takeaways. Perhaps the most essential one of all will be, you need to get on board if you want to be a world class team player. Don't be a lone ranger, if you want to be a game changer."

"Mate, give it a rest, eh?"

"Before we are forced to conclude this journey, mainly for the benefit of those people who still insist on the need to have lunch, there's just enough time for you to get on the same page and stand up and say this vital phrase out loud. Come on, do it with me," said the instructor, as he began marching on the spot and clapping his hands to every word. "There is no I in team, but there is in win. There is no I in team, but there is in win."

"I tell you what, mate. There's a 'U' in cunt and another one in fuck off."

"I beg your pardon," said the instructor, coming to a halt.

"It's all a load of bollocks. Total bullshit. So, why don't you just fuck off you cunt and stop wasting everybody's time?"

He then pushed the instructor more aggressively than he'd intended to and watched him go crashing into all the empty chairs in the front row. He was sure the bloke was about to do something to him, he might've been wrong, but as far as he was concerned it had been self-defence. What he did know though, was that not one of his team-mates had offered to come to his assistance.

* * *

At long last, he heard the bleeping sound indicating that the train doors were closing, and the train was ready to depart. Only five stops and he would be home. At this time of day, no more than fifteen minutes. The trees and rooftops flashed by the window opposite like the fragments of recent events in his mind.

A large man wearing builder's clothes got on the train at the first stop, Bethnal Green, and sat in one of the many vacant, longitudinal seats opposite him. "HELLO, CAN YOU HEAR ME?" the builder shouted into his phone.

"YES, WE CAN," a woman shouted back from the next carriage, and a few people laughed.

The builder looked up and scowled, making eye contact with the only person opposite. "I'M ON A TRAIN," he continued, possibly even louder than before.

I could really do without this, thought the man. Out of the whole train why did this loud stupid builder come and sit opposite me. This is not doing my head any good at all. Four stops to go.

"NO! I'M ON A TRAIN, I'M GETTING OFF THE NEXT STOP," continued the builder to whoever he was in conversation with.

Thank fuck for that, thought the man. Peace and quiet for three stops at least. The train pulled into Cambridge Heath and the builder, true to his word, got up and left the train.

"I'M OFF THE TRAIN AND ON THE PLATFORM, NOW," said the builder, still audible on the train despite his new location.

Oh, for fuck's sake, thought the man, as the builder's replacement now sitting opposite him was a teenager playing loud, tinny sounding music from his phone. What the fuck is it with people? Haven't they got any consideration for others? Do they think nobody else can hear them? Or do they just not give a shit?

This was getting really annoying. He was starting to feel sick. He tried to suffer in silence but when the train stopped at the next station, London Fields, he said "Excuse me mate, haven't you got any headphones?

"No, I fucking haven't", the teenager replied.

"Could you turn it down a bit then? I've got a bad headache."

"No."

"Come on mate, it is a bit loud."

"Go and sit somewhere else if you don't like it"

"I can't, I don't feel well, and I was here first. Can't you do me a favour? I'm getting off in a couple of stops."

The teenager tried to turn it up even louder but when he realized it was already on full volume said, "Well, if you're getting off soon, it doesn't matter, does it. Anyway, what are you going to do about it if I don't turn it down?"

"Look mate, I really don't want any trouble. I'm not in the mood. I've had a bad day and I don't feel very well."

"Are you threatening me?"

"Eh? Didn't you just hear what I said?"

"Yeah, you said if you were in the mood, you'd give me trouble," snarled the teenager getting up from his seat.

The train had now pulled into Hackney Downs station. The man considered getting off, but he was only one stop from home. If he remained seated, not only would he feel a lot better, but he might also appear less intimidating to this teenager. A few more people were ready to get on at the platform but, once they had seen a teenager staring menacingly down at an ill looking man at the back of the last carriage, they quickly moved down the train.

The teenager then pressed his phone right up against the man's ear. This made the man stand up, if only to get away from the claustrophobic noise that was making the bile in his stomach rise towards his parched mouth. Before he had time to control himself, the man vomited acidic puke all down the teenager's light grey hoodie, even managing to get some on his matching jogging bottoms.

After the teenager had recovered from the initial shock of having someone throw up over him, he sat back down again, still not sure what he should do next. As his senses started to fully register the sight and smell around him, a retributory anger rose within his body. He stood up once again and made his way towards the man who, he noticed, was now looking a lot less like he was at death's door.

The man, wary of getting any puke on himself even if it was his own, wondered if there was any way he could somehow rationally fend off the looming teenager by way of civilized communication. Having quickly decided that there probably wasn't, his flying kung fu style kick landed powerfully in the teenager's stomach, forcing the teenager to slump back in his seat, and look on helplessly as his mobile phone was repeatedly stamped upon by his assailant.

He only stopped jumping up and down on the phone after he'd been overpowered by some of the other passengers and wrestled to the ground. He ceased to resist, even though he was now at his station. Somebody had pulled the emergency cord and no doubt the police were on their way. Would they believe that this had been an act of self-defence as well? He then remembered that he still had all the coke on him that he'd bought last night. What a terrible day, he should never have got out of bed. While lying there, pressed against the carriage floor, he noticed that his watch appeared to be broken. The glass which had previously covered its face was missing, and it looked like it only had one hand. Or, hopefully, the time was ten past two. Yes, that would probably be about right, he convinced himself.

Got To Score

Amanda looked at herself in the bedroom mirror as she applied her make-up. Better not put on too much, she thought, I don't want it to appear obvious that I'm on the pull. Amanda had a good feeling about tonight. She was ovulating and all she needed was some decent sperm inside her.

Having a baby was not a decision Amanda took lightly. She'd given this a lot of thought over the past few months and was now ready to take the plunge. She had a good job which was well paid, a nice flat in an up-and-coming area and a mother who would probably love a grandchild to look after whenever Amanda wanted her to. Plus, she was thirty-three now. That's no spring chicken in baby bearing years. As her friend Kelly had quite rightly pointed out to her, 'Her ovaries were a-knocking.' What was even better on a Thursday night, when your ovaries are a-knocking, and you're ovulating, was knowing that there would be a large selection of men guaranteed to be in your local pub, The Edgar Allan Poe on Stoke Newington Church Street.

It was tonight that England were playing against Egypt in something called the Italia 90 World Cup. Apparently, it was an important match, and a lot of people in the office where Amanda worked were talking about watching it. Even people who she would never have dreamt liked football, were harping on about this as if it were the only thing that really mattered in the world that day.

So, this was the plan: Go to the pub with Kelly, who, despite being a bit bewildered by Amanda's suggestion that they go and watch football, had fortunately agreed to go with her. She would then, hopefully, see a man in there she liked the look of. Someone of a similar calibre to herself. Attractive, but not stunning. Intelligent, though at the same time not a boffin. Considerate, while not necessarily being Bob Geldof. That sort of thing. Then, invite him back to her place, have sex and hey presto, Bob's your uncle and Fanny's your aunt, mission accomplished. Could it really be that simple? Despite having no idea what the chances of everything going according to plan were, Amanda thought they were good. She could feel it in her water.

Amanda had already decided that seeing the father again was irrelevant. If he turned out to be the man of her dreams, then that would obviously be a bonus. No, the intention was to have a consensual one-night stand where she would become pregnant, and he would never know or need to care. Amanda felt a wave of excitement come over her, not just because of what might lie ahead that night, but also due to a strong feeling of being in control of her life. There was a sense of power that she'd seldom felt before. Hopefully, whoever this guy is won't be like that Sting person and want to go on all night doing tantric sex before shooting his load. It would be much better if he was one of those 'splash & dash' types. That way she wouldn't have to have an embarrassing conversation with him the following morning or, perish the thought, make him breakfast. After all, she had to get up and go to work the next day.

Amanda's thoughts turned to her own conception. Her parents were already married, she'd seen the proof. She wondered what day of the week it had been, whether it had been during the day or night, if they had been drunk or stone cold sober and how long it had actually taken. She decided that her dad was probably not like Sting at all, but she liked to think he wasn't a 'splash & dash' man, either. Average, she reckoned, and left it at that.

Amanda knew full well why she was conceived, though. Her parents sat her down one Sunday afternoon, when she was sixteen, and broke the news to her that she had a half-brother from a previous relationship her dad had been in, before he'd ever met Amanda's mum. She'd been understandably shocked at first and then upset. There was a feeling of regret that she hadn't been able to grow up with an older brother and would never know what it would have been like not to be an only child. Would she have always had somebody to play with and share secrets? Though, maybe they wouldn't have got along. She'd heard a lot about sibling rivalry, and this might have been the case with him, especially as they weren't fully related. Anyway, it was immaterial now. There was no way of finding him and she wasn't entirely sure that she wanted to anymore, even if she could.

She knew his name was Kevin, but he probably didn't use her father's surname, Dixon. Or maybe he did. No, more likely to use his mother's surname. What was it? Burton, that's it. Or perhaps he has a new stepfather and uses that person's surname, which could be anything. Anyway, there must be thousands of Kevins out there and hundreds of Dixons and Burtons as well. What am I supposed to do, put an advert in Loot, she thought? Something like, 'Woman looking for lost half-brother who might go by the surname Burton or Dixon or something else entirely different. First name Kevin. Purpose of wanting to meet - curiosity to see whether they would have got on with each other when they were children.'

It must have been terrible for her dad, and her mum as well, she decided, when this woman who was Kevin's mother took him away from them. Apparently, the boy had lived with Amanda's mum & dad for about five or six months after being presented to them, unexpectedly, when he was a year old. Kevin's mother had been struggling financially and thought he'd have a better life if his real father brought him up. The real mother then decided she wanted him back for good and took him away. Neither Amanda's father, nor her mother, ever saw him again and Amanda was born less than a year later.

Who needs brothers and sisters anyway? Amanda had grown up alright on her own and her baby would as well. Even if he or she wouldn't necessarily have a father around, either. Who needs a relationship to have a family, anyway? Since splitting up with her long-term partner, Chris, almost eighteen months ago, Amanda had become quite cynical about relationships in general. Chris had never wanted to commit and had shown no intention of wanting to start a family, despite the fact that they had been together for eight years. Amanda had loved him and wasn't unhappy in any way but had just felt that there must be more to life than the one she had, and Chris was obviously feeling the same way. They inevitably drifted apart. They sold their flat before the big property crash and, after moving in with her mother for a little while to let the dust settle, she was able to afford a flat of her own.

Amanda eventually met a few men and had some short-term relationships, all of which ended miserably. Meeting the perfect partner was the hardest thing in the world, Amanda had decided. First, you have to meet somebody you were attracted to, usually physically to start off with, then mentally. After that, you need to find out if that person has enough in common with you to keep the relationship going once the initial excitement has worn off. Next up was that you had to fall in love with that person, adore everything about them, and want to do anything you possibly could to make them happy as well as be certain that you wanted to spend the rest of your life with them. Once you've done all that, you've then got to hope that person will feel exactly the same way about you. What are the chances of that happening? No wonder it was difficult. Most people, she suspected, just accepted that this was very unlikely to happen, gave up trying to find the perfect partner, and decided to settle for what they've got to avoid a lifetime of celibacy and loneliness.

Amanda decided that she would make sure she devoted all her love and affection towards her child instead. Firstly, though, she had to concentrate on the task at hand, which was conceiving by having sexual intercourse with somebody of the opposite sex.

Amanda chose a t-shirt which wasn't too revealing and a skirt which wasn't too short. It had taken a long time, but she was certain she'd made the right choice and that she looked good without appearing desperate. After considering her jewelry box, she quickly dismissed the idea. Tonight, was definitely not the night for a pearl necklace. She was all ready to go and right on cue, her doorbell rang.

"I can't believe we are going to a pub to watch football," said Kelly, walking into Amanda's flat. "Since when have you become a football supporter?"

"It'll be a laugh," Amanda replied. "Everyone at work is talking about watching the match tonight, I don't want to feel like I missed out on something when they all start discussing it tomorrow, do I?"

"But it's going to be full of horrible, smelly, drunk, shouty blokes."

"Not the pub we're going to, it won't. You saw the type of people that were in there last Saturday night when we walked by when England were about to play football. There were quite a few women in there to watch the match as well, and the men looked totally different from the usual football fans. Some of them looked like they might actually be able to read and write."

"They were still noisy, though. Singing along to that song by that fat, bald singer. You know, Whatsisname? Not Buster Bloodvessel, the other bloke, the one who's Italian."

"Do you mean Pavarotti? That just proves what a better class of football supporter you get now. People who appreciate good opera."

"We won't be able to hear each other talk."

"We're not going there to talk. We're going to watch England play footy. That's what Alex at work says people like us are calling it now. Everyone says it's completely changed and it's alright for respectable people to follow footy now, not just illiterate thugs and riff-raff."

* * *

When Amanda and Kelly arrived at the pub at a quarter to eight, it was already busy despite there still being fifteen minutes until kick-off. They had just been served their drinks at the bar when nearly everybody in the pub started singing God Save The Queen. The TV pictures were showing the England players singing along patriotically.

"Who are those bunch of munters?" asked Kelly.

"That's us," Amanda replied. "They're singing our national anthem, so it must be."

"They look like a load of village idiots that have been rounded up for the night."

Amanda was just about to disagree but then she thought, actually, Kelly might have a point.

"What country are these care in the community people playing football against, anyway?" Kelly enquired.

"Egypt."

"Egypt? Do they play football?"

"Of course, they do. Everybody does," Amanda replied. "Alex at work said even the Faroe Islands play footy now."

"The Faroe Islands? Isn't that the same thing as Egypt?"

"No, of course not."

"I know that. It was a joke. They're either those ones in Scotland or the ones near the Falklands, in Argentina?"

"Let's just watch the match," said Amanda, as she looked around the pub for potential sexual partners.

"This isn't exactly very exciting," said Kelly after an extremely dull first half. "Is it supposed to be like this? If it is, I don't think I'll bother watching any more football matches."

A man who had caught Amanda's eye earlier was now standing next to her at the bar, having just been served

"Are you enjoying the footy?" he said to Amanda. "It's not a great game, is it?"

"What, footy isn't? How come you're watching it then if you don't like the game?" Amanda replied.

"No, I meant the match isn't great, is it? It's tense though, we've got to score."

"Definitely. What do you reckon our chances are?" asked Amanda.

Before the man had a chance to answer, they were interrupted by someone who appeared to be a friend of the man Amanda had now decided was the most likely candidate to be the father of her future child.

"Oi Rich, stop chatting up the ladies and get those beers over here, at the double. And that's an order," the man's friend shouted, before turning round and returning to where he'd been standing earlier.

"Sorry about that," said the man. "I'm Rich, by the way."

"That's good, you can buy us both a drink then," said Kelly.

"No, I mean everyone calls me Rich, as in its short for Richard," said Rich. "I'd better take these drinks over. Let's hope it's a better second half and we win, eh? And then we can have something to celebrate. I'll definitely buy you both a drink then."

"He was quite nice," Amanda said, once the man had gone.

"I don't know, he seemed like a bit of a dick to me," replied Kelly. "And his mate is a complete nob."

Amanda looked over to where Rich and his friend were standing and noticed that he was looking directly at her. He smiled and raised his pint glass. Amanda smiled back and raised her hand to show that she had her fingers crossed.

Ten minutes into the second half when there still hadn't been any improvement in the entertainment on show, Kelly said, "I'm sorry but I think I'm going to go. This is boring the tits off me."

"Okay. If you're sure," said Amanda, trying not to sound too relieved.

"What, you don't mind?"

"No, it's alright. If you're not enjoying yourself, it's no point staying here. You head off. I'll be fine. I think I'll just stay and see what happens."

Once Kelly had gone, Amanda tried to pay more attention to what was going on in the game. England had something called a free kick, the commentator announced.

The player who she'd earlier thought looked most like a village idiot was preparing to take it. People all around the pub were shouting out various instructions.

"Put a decent ball in this time."

"Let's make this one count"

"Put your laces through it and stick it in the onion bag."

"Kick the ball in the goal."

Almost as if they had magically heard the shouts of encouragement coming from the pub, England scored a goal. Everybody in the pub was jumping up and down and cheering. They had instantly become happy and carefree, and Amanda decided to join in as well.

When things had calmed down a little, she looked over to where the man Rich was standing. He smiled at her and again raised his glass. Amanda smiled back and this time she raised a triumphant clenched fist.

At long last, thirty minutes later, which had seemed like an entire day at work to Amanda, the match was over. England had won, one-nil. Everyone was cheering. Lots of people rushed to the bar to get another drink and quite a few people decided they'd had enough excitement for one Thursday night and charged out of the pub.

"Eng-er-land, Eng-er-land, Eng-er-land" was being sung loudly by those who remained. The owner of the pub decided to put on loud, uplifting music from that week's pop charts, in an attempt to keep the party going.

Rich was coming over towards Amanda, smiling broadly. "I'll buy you that drink now, if you want," he said.

"Thanks, that'd be lovely. We've got to celebrate, haven't we? Whoo-hoo!" Amanda replied.

"Where's your friend, has she gone?"

"Yes, she's not into footy as much as me. What about yours?"

"Yeah, he's gone as well. He has to be in work early tomorrow to make a load of people redundant. Right, let's get some more drinks in and some shots. And let's party! It's not every day you beat Egypt, get to the quarter finals of the World Cup and meet an attractive young lady who loves footy."

An hour later, after more drinks and more shots, Amanda and Rich were still partying hard. They were wildly jumping up and down to the music, and both of them had their index fingers pointing towards their genitals as they sang along at the top of their voices to MC Hammer's 'U Can't Touch This.' Then they started kissing passionately. This was going even better than expected, thought Amanda.

Inevitably, once the pub had closed, Rich had gone back with Amanda to her flat. Amanda was relieved that Rich hadn't been a splash and dash man after all, and as he wasn't in any way like Sting either, she'd enjoyed what had been an extremely fulfilling experience. They had both passed out in each other's arms afterwards. She was even glad that Rich had ended up staying the night. It was so nice to wake up with somebody she liked, again.

"Good morning, lovely," said Rich, laughing. "I'm sorry, I'm sure you did tell me, but I think I've forgotten your name?"

"That's alright, I think you might have had one or two other penetrating thoughts on your mind," Amanda laughed. "It's Amanda. I remember yours. It's Rich, isn't it?"

"Yeah, my mates all call me Rich. It got shortened from Richard, which they started calling me because I used to live in Wales and my surname is Burton. And it just stuck. That's not my real name, though. My real name is Kevin."

What are the chances of that happening? Amanda wondered, before silently getting out of bed and heading towards the bathroom to be violently sick.

Love At First Bite

Melissa was excited; it was Saturday, and she was going on a date that evening. These cold, damp, prematurely dark afternoons usually depressed her as she very rarely had anything good to look forward to. Often, this feeling carried over into Sunday and by Monday morning she was glad to be going back to work again. At least then she would be able to talk to somebody. On more than one occasion, the first person she'd had a real conversation with on Monday morning also happened to be the last person she'd had one with on the previous Friday afternoon. She dreaded the thought of not having a job as this might mean her not actually conversing with anybody for weeks or months on end. Maybe even forever.

The fear of this becoming a reality had finally persuaded Melissa to join a dating site. She had always been against the idea and romantically hoped that fate would ensure that she would eventually find true love, or that true love would find her. As of yet though, this hadn't been the case. She had heard that love hides in mysterious places, but she hadn't encountered it on the train, either to or from the office where she worked, in the supermarket where she shopped, or in the park where she escaped when she felt the walls closing in on her. Those were probably the only places it could happen, unless some stranger unexpectedly knocked on her door one day and said, 'I love you', which was highly unlikely, even for those people who were far more attractive than Melissa.

It wasn't that Melissa was unattractive, but she always regarded her looks to be those of a person that somebody probably *would* kick out of bed for eating crisps. Not that Melissa ever ate anything in bed, she always considered the whole concept to be very peculiar. Perhaps, if she met a nice man and he brought her breakfast in bed one morning, then she might give it a go. Hopefully, though, it would be something a bit more substantial than just a packet of crisps. She could then tell all the people she worked with how thoughtful and kind her new boyfriend was and how he had surprised her by bringing her a delicious breakfast in bed served on a tray. There would be a small cafetiere of freshly ground coffee, a glass of hand squeezed orange juice, an oven baked flaky warm croissant, a very tiny dish filled with some artisan strawberry jam and maybe a delicate little vase with a flower in it. Now something like that would really impress people and everybody would say how lovely that was and probably be a little envious. It then occurred to her that if it was acceptable to have breakfast in bed, why didn't the same apply to lunch or dinner? If she were to tell people that her new boyfriend had brought her a roast dinner with all the trimmings in bed instead, it would have completely the opposite effect on them, however appetizing her description of the meal happened to be.

There were the occasional days though, when Melissa looked in the mirror and thought she did look quite attractive, but these were far outnumbered by the many days in which she didn't. Fortunately, Melissa had a very good photograph of herself which had been taken on one of those rare, good hair and good face days. This was the one she chose to upload on to the dating site about a month or so ago, just as the dreaded onslaught of winter was about to make its inevitable return, bringing with it those suicidal thoughts that had previously frightened the life out of her.

Choosing a suitable dating site had been difficult. Melissa was reluctant to ask anybody for any recommendations, as she was still struggling with the shame that she associated with having to resort to such methods. All of her old friends had been married for several years now and had children, so she was fairly sure that they wouldn't be up to speed on which sites happened to be the most favourable. She certainly didn't want anybody at work to know she was considering online dating, so she set out to investigate all alone. She was surprised by how many of these places existed and how specific they all were. There were sites for lovers of cats, dogs and all sorts of animals. There was even one for music lovers. While Melissa was tempted by the idea of sharing a favourite album to see if you were compatible, she was extremely doubtful that there would be anybody else out there who also rated Modern Romance's The Platinum Collection as the greatest album of all time.

So finally, after spending many long nights wading through the minefield of internet dating sites, Melissa chose one which she thought was most suitable. A pizza based one where you are matched by your favourite toppings.

Melissa's initial excitement was now turning to panic. She had tried on and rejected nearly everything from her winter wardrobe at least twice and still couldn't decide what to wear. A small mountain of clothes lay on the bed and Melissa, standing there in just her new underwear, wondered whatever had possessed her to buy some of these things. At last, she opted for the charcoal grey roll neck jumper with black trousers and black boots. It had been the first outfit she had tried on just over two hours ago, but sometimes, you really do need to try on everything else you own just to be certain that your first instincts were right all along.

Looking out of her window, Melissa could see that the weather had deteriorated. The rain was falling extremely hard and, judging by the way the trees were swaying, there must be a raging wind blowing as well. All the cab options she tried were hopeless and, even if she were to book the earliest one available, this would undoubtedly result in her arriving late. Melissa certainly didn't want to take the chance that her date would patiently sit and wait for her. There was only one thing for it, she would have to drive.

Melissa put on her raincoat, grabbed an umbrella, picked up her car keys and ran out into the howling wind and violent rain towards her car. The few minutes it had taken to get from her front door to her car seat might have been enough to dampen the lower half of her trousers, but certainly not her enthusiasm. She typed in the destination 'Citta del Diavolo Pizzeria, Lower Clapton' in to her sat-nav and was reliably informed that the journey would take thirteen minutes. Melissa had never been to Clapton before, Upper or Lower, despite it being in the same borough in which she lived, and this made her feel like she was undertaking a new adventure. Her date, Dave from Leyton, had suggested Lower Clapton as he said it was about half way between where they both lived and, as they were both such massive pizza fiends, he knew just the place to go for a bite to eat.

I've missed this, thought Melissa, as she drove through the storm-lashed streets of North East London. The anticipation as you travel to meet somebody, knowing that they are looking forward to seeing you as much as you are of seeing them. Spending an evening talking and laughing together, content in each other's company with neither party wanting to be anywhere else on earth.

Melissa reached her destination and conveniently parked her car close by in the surprisingly quiet street. She took a deep breath and, despite the torrential rain, walked slowly towards the Pizzeria with just her insecure umbrella for protection. She apprehensively opened the restaurant door and was at once struck by the unmistakable smell of garlic. Who wouldn't appreciate such an aroma? Melissa thought, as she began to salivate. Vampires, perhaps? But Melissa hoped that, unlike most people she had previously encountered, she did not have any vampiric qualities.

"Hello, we have a reservation for a table for two at 8.30pm, in the name of Dave. I'm not sure if the gentleman is already here," Melissa said, precisely the way she had practiced the line over and over in her head as she walked from her car to the restaurant.

"Ah, benvenuta Signora, please come in," said a man dressed from head to toe in black. "Let me just put on my glasses and I shall look in the book."

"Yes, of course." Melissa replied, hoping her voice did not betray the feeling of trepidation she was so desperate to conceal. "You probably haven't noticed, but I actually wear contact lenses. Without them I would literally be as blind as a bat," she continued, before laughing more wildly than was perhaps acceptable.

The man opened a large, claret coloured, leather journal and, with a slight frown as he concentrated on running his finger down the page, said, "Let me see now, Dave, Dave, Dave, Dave, ah yes, Dave 8.30. Please come with me."

Melissa was taken to a small plastic table which, like all the other tables in the Pizzeria, was disappointingly unoccupied.

"Per favore," he said, motioning Melissa to be seated. "Would the Signora like a drink while she is waiting?"

"Just some sparkling water, please."

"Maybe Giuseppe brings the big bottle of sparkling water for the Signora, no?" smiled the man.

"Yes, why not. Let's go crazy," Melissa smiled back.

Melissa looked at her watch. It was 8.36. Nothing to worry about, she decided. She checked her phone but there were no messages. I'm only a few minutes late, she thought, surely Dave would have waited at least that long for her if he had arrived on time. Plus, the waiter would have mentioned something, probably along the lines of, 'Oh yes, the Signore Dave was here at exactly 8.30 but when he saw that the Signora had not turned up, he was very sad and left immediately.' No, he must have got caught up in traffic or something. The weather was still horrendous. She would wait a little while longer and then maybe send him a text, just to let him know she was safely at the pizzeria and to enquire what time he thought he would arrive.

Melissa wasn't relaxed sitting on her own in a public place. It made her feel self-conscious that people might think she had no friends. Not that there were any other people eating in the pizzeria, but there was a good chance that the waiter might have been suspicious. Right on cue though, the waiter returned carrying a large bottle of sparkling water and two glasses. This at least, made Melissa feel a little better. He obviously did believe that she was supposed to be meeting somebody else in there and hadn't made up some fictitious person just to prove that she wasn't all alone on a Saturday night.

"Maybe the Signora would like to look at the menu, showing all of our bellissimo pizzas, while she waits," said the waiter passing her a large, laminated card. "We were very busy earlier, just as it started to get dark. The special today was stuffed hearts with steak, but that is all finished. Also, as it is now illegal, we can't allow anybody in here to have the capon," he added, before retreating discreetly.

Love At First Bite

The waiter obviously feels sorry for me now and wants to give me something to read, thought Melissa, becoming more agitated. He'll probably come over with a trolley containing a selection of books and magazines if I'm here on my own much longer, she imagined. After reading every item on the menu at least four times she took another look at her watch. It was now nine o'clock.

Melissa's anxiety had now reached a level where uninvited thoughts flew erratically around her troubled mind. Silently, she began to reflect: Okay, half an hour is a reasonable time to expect somebody to send a message saying they will be late, isn't it? Though, to be honest, fifteen minutes would have been polite. Perhaps I should just leave and forget the whole thing. That way if he hasn't bothered to turn up for a pizza, I won't either. Two can play that game. If he's changed his mind about meeting me, why didn't he just tell me, rather than make me drive all the way over to a place I've never been to before, in a storm, just to sit on my own in an empty pizzeria wondering if anybody is ever going to turn up. Why can't people just be honest with each other? We all know none of us are going to get out of this miserable existence alive and, as much as we try and deny it, none of us are going to live forever, so you'd think everybody would be much more considerate, look after each other a lot more and care about people's feelings. But no, it's the exact opposite. Everybody is only interested in thinking about themselves. He probably would have turned out to be exactly like all the rest anyway. Taking everything he could get out of me, bleeding me dry, before eventually discarding me and moving on to somebody else. Why couldn't you be different, Dave from Leyton? Maybe he is different. Or was. Perhaps he's dead. Or he's had an accident and is in hospital. He might have been rushing to get here on time because he couldn't wait to see me and got run over attempting to cross a busy road as he darted in between the speeding traffic coming from both directions. What do I do, then? Why is everything so difficult? Why can't I just have a nice evening with somebody and be happy like everybody else out there?

Melissa let out a piercing scream as she exhumed what seemed like more than a lifetime's worth of frustration from the darkest depths of her mind. She sat staring blankly, tears falling down her face like raindrops on a window that needs to be rehabilitated.

The waiter slowly made his way over to where Melissa was sitting. "Is everything alright with the Signora?" he asked. Without waiting for an answer, he cocked his head to the left and smiled, "It is a bad sign when you see somebody's cross in the restaurant. Maybe the Signora is hungry and would like some garlic dough balls while she is waiting."

Melissa didn't reply and continued to stare straight ahead, deep in thought, trying to solve a conundrum she knew she would never have the answer to. The waiter quickly reappeared with the garlic dough balls, along with an enormous wooden black pepper mill. "Here, especially for the Signora, the specialty of the house. Guaranteed to make the Signora look beautiful and feel very happy again. Buon appetito."

When the waiter returned a short time later, he could see that Melissa had not touched the food, nor had she altered her position. He was now extremely concerned and said, "Would the Signora like to talk about anything? I can sit down here with you if that would help."

"Yes, please. I don't want to keep sitting on my own anymore and I really don't know what to do," Melissa sobbed.

"Please try not to cry. You look much prettier when you are not crying. Did you contact the Signore Dave who you were meeting?"

"There's no point. There's a strong possibility that he no longer exists."

"Perhaps you would feel better if you were to go home. Should I phone a cab for you?"

"No, I have my car with me. It's alright, I will leave soon. Just talk to me for a little bit longer while I sit here, please."

"Of course. Take as long as you like. Are you sure you will be alright driving home? Do you have far to go?"

"Not too far. Just at the back of Abney Park Cemetry, Stoke Newington. About thirteen minutes away. You are very kind, thank you."

"That is on the way to where I live. Maybe it's best that you leave your car here. We can get the number 106 bus together, and you can come and get your car tomorrow when you are feeling much better."

"No, I'll be fine. Thank you so much for caring about me. I'd almost forgotten what that feels like. It really is lovely of you. It has been a strange night, but I feel so comfortable sitting here talking to you. It's almost as if we have some sort of connection. Tell me, what do you think of Modern Romance?"

"Ah, yes," the waiter sighed. Then with a wistful look on his face, continued, "This is not easy like ABC. All I can say is, even if it seems very difficult sometimes, people like us should never give up believing in modern romance and knowing that it is still possible for them to make beautiful music together. But perhaps, it is also not for everyone," he smiled gently.

"Yes! I just knew you would say that," said Melissa. "Come on. Let me drive you home."

He turned off the lights and locked the door to the Pizzeria. The earlier storm had now subsided. They walked in silence towards Melissa's car and got in. As Melissa turned the ignition key, the car was filled with the unmistakable sound of the Modern Romance classic 'Ay Ay Ay Ay Moosey' playing in the car's CD player. Melissa looked across and gave a huge smile to this mysterious man she couldn't quite believe she'd been lucky enough to meet.

The man smiled back politely, clutching a white paper bag lined with silver foil. Inside it contained the garlic dough balls he had earlier offered to Melissa. Maybe the Signora could have them in the morning when she has her breakfast in bed, he thought. Though, if she still doesn't want them, I'll have them, he decided.

Nicker In A Twist

It was the last day of the football season and The Castle pub, situated in a backstreet in Haggerston, was surprisingly quiet.

"I know it's pissing down with rain out there, but I thought it'd be busier than this," said Julie, as she stood facing three men who were all seated at a table. "Shall I get the Britney Spears in?" she enquired.

"It's alright, I've just gone and got the Dame Edna's. Let me get you one," said Ray, hauling himself up from his overburdened chair. "What are you having, your usual? A Nelson Mandela?"

"Yes please. Thanks," replied Julie.

"Your wish is my command," Ray announced, before standing in front of Julie and pointing down at his feet with his chubby index fingers. "Hey Julie, do you like my new Adidas Gloria Gaynors?" Without waiting for an answer, he continued to waddle off towards to the bar.

"They're very nice. They take years off you," Julie called over to the retreating Ray.

Then, turning on a sixpence, which surprisingly for a man of his frame he was able to do quite gracefully, Ray enquired, "A pint, yeah?"

"Of course, if that's allowed," smiled Julie. "Who else is coming then?" she continued, as she sat down in the spare seat, next to Pete, at the table.

"I think it's just us four," said Pete. "All the others know they've got no chance of winning, so none of them can be arsed to come down."

"I hope they've already coughed up the bangers and mash, then," said Terry, from across the table.

"Yep, Ray's got it all sorted. One of us is going to rack up seven hundred and fifty nicker after 6pm tonight. Winner takes all. No second, third or even fourth place trophy," confirmed Pete.

Back in mid-August, on the eve of a new football season, fifteen people handed in a list of their predictions showing where they thought each of the twenty clubs in the Premier League would finish in the final table, from top all the way down to the bottom. The entry was fifty pounds per person, meaning, whoever won would make a profit of seven hundred pounds. There had been a fixed group of fourteen men who had been doing this every season for the past few years, and when Ray had mentioned to the others that Julie was interested in joining as well, there had been more than the odd rumble of discontent. Terry was by no means the only one who had pointed out that Julie was a woman and therefore shouldn't be allowed to join, but he did seem to be the one who had contested this most vehemently.

"Julie can't join, she's a bird. We can't have birds in it. It's just for blokes," Terry had said.

"Why not? You know she knows her football. And if you reckon you know more than she does, then it's another fifty quid in the pot," Ray had replied.

Eventually, Ray's logic had persuaded everybody to accept Julie into the competition, although this did not mean that everybody was entirely happy about it.

"Alright then, but I ain't entirely happy about it," Terry had said, and had just left it at that.

Ray came back with Julie's pint of Stella and once he was seated said, "I was just telling everyone before you got here Julie, you're in pole position."

"You like doing pole position don't you Julie?" said Terry, laughing.

"Yeah, it's my favourite," Julie replied, shaking her head slowly from left to right.

"What's your second favourite, the ironing board or the washing machine?" Terry continued. This time with a contemptuous smile.

"What's the matter with you? Can't you handle getting beaten by a woman?" asked Pete.

"It ain't over yet. Let's see what happens in this afternoon's games first," Terry replied.

Ray decided it was time for him to clarify the situation as best he could and pulled out a tattered exercise book before giving the following statement: "It was pretty close up until this week and then Wolves did you a massive Cheesy Quaver Julie, when they done The Hamsters in their own back yard at the Olympic Stadium. So, as long as Villa, Southampton and United don't lose their games at home, and Leeds don't get anything away against Man-Qatar City, it should probably be yours for the taking. Otherwise, you'll need Palace not to get turned over by the Mickey Mousers and Brighton not to get a result at Leicester or Pete could be in with a good chance of winning, depending on goal difference in all the other games as well, of course. Terry, you want the complete opposite of everything that Julie needs to happen."

"We'll see," said Terry, as he lifted his pint glass towards him, being careful not to touch it with his little finger.

Julie kept quiet. I will do my talking on the pitch, she thought. Or in the tattered exercise book, at any rate.

"Are you definitely renewing your season ticket, Julie?" Pete said, changing the subject slightly.

"Yeah, I suppose so," Julie sighed. "Can't say I'm over confident about next season, though. But let's see who we buy in the summer.

It'd better not be any more sloppy seconds from Chelsea. What about you?"

"Yeah, the same," said Pete. "It's habit, isn't it? Like an addiction. Though I think that I might enjoy going a lot more if I didn't hate as many of our players as much as I do."

"You ain't joking," said Julie. "Have you seen the latest pictures of them tossers advertising the new kits for next season? They're all wearing loads of their own fucking bling. Gold chains and earrings all over the shop. I thought our new sponsor was H. Samuel for a minute. What's all that about?"

"Tell me about it. It's not like we don't know they're all millionaires, is it? They don't have to rub our fucking noses in it. Who do they think they are anyway? Them useless bunch of twats finished mid table two years running."

"And they're still charging us the highest ticket prices in the world to watch a load of mediocre bollocks."

"Yeah, we've been ripped off for years to make those fucker's rich," said Pete. "I don't know, sometimes, I ask myself the same question as that little foreign, raspberry kid on the anti-discrimination advert, when he goes 'Why do we like football?' Anyway, look on the positive side, if you win this today, that's about three quarters of your season ticket in your sky rocket."

"Fuck that," Julie replied. "I've already sorted out an interest free loan for the season ticket, like I usually do. No, if I win the seven hundred and fifty, that's going straight towards a good holiday."

"You got anywhere in mind?" asked Pete.

"No. I haven't really thought about it yet. Somewhere nice, though."

"Anyway, really glad you're renewing, Julie. It's always lovely meeting up with you after the game for a booze."

"Yeah, absolutely. We're usually in desperate need of one after watching that load of old rubbish."

"Thank fuck we're playing away today," said Pete. "I've had more than enough of going over there for one season. Though, I bet come August, we'll have forgotten all about it and we'll be like a rat up a drainpipe when it's time to go over there again."

Terry, who had been interrogating Ray about the validity of his calculations, stood up and said, "I suppose I'd better get a drink in if Julie doesn't have to go to the bar,"

"Julie offered to get a drink when she came in," said Pete. "You haven't bought one yet anyway, have you?"

"Alright, I'll get them in," replied Terry. "What can I get you Julie, a nice Babycham?"

"No, another pint is fine, thanks," Julie replied, suppressing most of her anger. "That is, if you don't mind too much," she added.

Terry laughed to himself as he made his way to the bar to get the drinks.

"I don't know what's the matter with that nobhead these days?" said Julie.

"Just ignore him," said Pete. "He didn't want women to be allowed in this competition in the first place, and now he's got the right 'ump because he's losing to you, as well."

"I don't understand what's he got against women being in it."

"I reckon he's probably scared of them," said Ray. "Maybe it's because he's only got a tiny Jermaine Jenas."

The three of them were still laughing as Terry returned with the drinks. He suspected they were laughing at something to do with him but, not wanting to appear paranoid, he kept quiet and sat down. We'll see who's laughing later, he thought to himself, as he took a sip of his drink.

It was the only day of the entire football season when all ten matches kicked off simultaneously. This was to ensure that nobody had an advantage over anybody else by knowing exactly what they did, or didn't, have to do. So, once 4pm finally came around on this unseasonably wet Sunday afternoon in May, they all sat nervously in front of the pub's large TV screen, and over the course of the next two hours, watched the scores of all the matches get regularly updated.

After more twists and turns than you would find in a whole series of Roald Dahl's 'Tales of the Unexpected', all ten matches were over, and the final Premier League Table for that season was ready to be cemented in to the annals of history.

"Go figure Ray, you do the math," Ray said, in a poorly imitated American accent. He said the same thing every year, around about the same time, although he assumed everybody was always far too tense to actually laugh at his joke. Despite the fact nobody ever laughed, it wouldn't deter him from trying it again the following year, and he hoped that it at least brought a little light relief to the proceedings. Out came his tattered exercise book, and off he went to find a quiet corner somewhere in the pub to enable him to do lots of complicated calculations without any unwanted distractions.

Twenty-five minutes later Ray returned, holding his tattered exercise book aloft. He had a look on his face that suggested the contents in his hand may very well hold the entire secrets of the known universe. "Ze results are in," he said, for some reason only known to him, in a terrible German accent. "Und zee vinner is," he continued, before doing an embarrassingly bad impression of a drum roll sound, and momentarily pausing for dramatic effect. He then resumed the attempted drum roll sound, imagining how much his friends appreciated the way he first built up and then stretched out the tension. There was a hushed silence before he dramatically took a deep breath and said, "Wait for it...., wait for it...."

"Just fucking tell us who won, you fucking fat cunt!" shouted Terry,

"Alright, alright, don't get your knickers in a twist. It's Julie. Julie's the winner!" Ray said, deciding to abandon his proposed plan for a simulation of fanfare trumpets just for this year.

"Are you fucking Bobby Moore?" enquired Terry.

"Yes, of course I am. I've double checked. And Pete, you were second. You just missed out by five points," said Ray, before adding, in an attempted Geordie accent mimicking the commentator from Bullseye, "Un-lucky."

"Well done, Julie," said Pete. "I'm really pleased for you."

"Fucking beginners' luck," said Terry.

"Of course, it ain't," said Pete. "How can it be? It isn't a sweepstake, or like the football pools and the Lottery where you just put down a load numbers that are dates of people's anniversaries and birthdays. You have to know your stuff. The league table doesn't lie. Just admit that Julie knows her onions when it comes to football and a lot more about it than you do."

"Bollocks," Terry said, deciding there was no need for any further elaboration.

Julie, in the meantime, decided to sit quietly as she was still in a very minor state of shock. The only woman, amongst fourteen men, and she had won. It felt incredibly good, and there was the added bonus of being able to trouser seven hundred and fifty pounds as well. But right now, the best part of winning was the look on Terry's face.

"You can go and buy yourself a new handbag now, can't you?" sneered Terry.

"I might have to buy a bigger purse first, so I can fit in all the money I've won off you and your mates," Julie smiled.

"Are you going to buy us all a drink with your winnings then?" asked Terry.

"Sure, Babycham for everyone." Julie declared, determined not to let Terry ruin her happiness in any way, shape or form that evening.

Are you lot staying here all night getting off your tits?" Terry asked an hour or so later. "Because I ain't, I'm Frank Bough. Some of us have got to get up for work at four thirty in the morning."

"Well, we haven't and it's still early," everybody else agreed.

Terry stormed out of the pub. He didn't bother saying good night or wish anybody an enjoyable rest of the evening. Even if he did have other things on his mind, there really is no excuse for rudeness.

When the pub was about to close, Julie, Ray and Pete gathered up their belongings and headed outside back to, what they had now come to accept as, reality. Their two days of freedom for that week were over. Inevitably, their miserable, time-consuming, personality-suppressing and soul-destroying jobs were waiting for them the following morning; enabling them to attempt to make somebody else rich and possibly happy, while they, in the meantime, unwittingly wished their lives away.

"I am proper Lee Marvin?" announced Ray. "It must be all that excitement. Who wants to get something to eat?"

"You'll get turned away if you try and order any food somewhere. I can just see them saying 'Sorry mate, I think you've had enough, already,'" Pete replied.

"Yeah, especially if it's one of them 'All You Can Eat' buffet places," Julie added.

"I bet everyone in there would shit themselves if they saw him come walking through the door," said Pete.

"They'd probably throw him out and then give him a good kicking just to make sure he doesn't try and come back in," added Julie, now really starting to get into the swing of things.

"Alright, alright, I am still here you know," said Ray. "I think you've both made your point. It's not my fault that I'm big boned."

"The only big bones you've ever had are from those dodgy drumsticks you get out of that Tasty Hot Fried Chicken shit-hole you go to down the road," replied Pete, as he and Julie carried on laughing.

"I take it I can't persuade either of you then?" Ray said, conceding defeat.

"No, I'm going home. Thanks a lot, anyway. And thanks again for sorting everything out today," said Julie.

"The pleasure was all mine. And well done again for winning. You should be really proud," said Ray, giving Julie a heartfelt smile and a histrionic salute.

"Sorry, mate. I'm going to call it a day as well," Pete said, before turning to face Julie. "I had better walk back with you, just in case any wrong 'uns saw you with all that money Ray gave you."

After saying goodbye to Ray, Pete and Julie walked along the pleasantly quiet High Street. The rain had now stopped, and without too many other people about, they could both fully appreciate the comforting familiarity of an area they had all of their lives referred to as home.

"Thanks for walking back with me Pete, and I appreciate you sticking up for me this afternoon. You didn't have to, though."

"Yeah, I know you can look after yourself, but you know how much you mean to me, don't you? Just because of what happened between us, and everything that's changed since then, it doesn't mean I don't still care about you."

"I know you do. Thanks for being such a great friend."

"That's alright. I'll always be here for you, you know that."

They had now arrived at Julie's front gate, and they held each other in a warm embrace.

"See you in August for that drink after the first game of the new season," smiled Julie.

"Definitely. I'm looking forward to it. The drink that is, not the football," Pete laughed.

"The glory days might be coming back Pete, you never know."

"I think you had better lay off that Babycham if it's going to make you talk bollocks."

"I've never had a Babycham in my life. Anyway, you know me, I don't need Babycham to talk bollocks. You take care now."

"You too. And are you sure he's going to be alright with you when you get in?" said Pete. Even after all these years, he still couldn't bring himself to say Julie's husband's name.

"I'm sure he will. He'll be asleep now. You heard what he said, he's got to get up at four thirty in the morning."

Tunnel Vision

He arrived at The Daniel Defoe pub on Stoke Newington Church Street, fifteen minutes before they had arranged to meet, and ordered himself a drink.

"The Estrella is off at the moment, I've just got to change the barrel," said the young woman behind the bar. "If you want to take a seat, I'll bring it over to you when it's ready," she suggested.

He found an empty table in an area of the pub which could easily be seen from the front door. A few minutes later the young woman from behind the bar came over, placed a pint on his table, and pointed the card machine in his direction. After paying, he thanked her for her help, and she gave him a big smile before saying, "Enjoy."

He watched her return to her position behind the bar as he took a sip of his drink. Then he took another soon after. After pausing very briefly, he had another sip. It didn't taste right but maybe it was just him, as he hadn't had a drink since Sunday, which was four days ago. After taking yet another sip, he decided that there was definitely something strange about the way it tasted. He got up and walked over to the bar carrying his glass which was now a quarter empty.

"Excuse me," he said to the woman who had served him. "This tastes a bit funny. Is this Estrella?"

"No, it's Budweiser, I think."

"But I ordered Estrella, and you said you were changing the barrel."

"Yeah, but I don't know how to do it on my own, I'm going to have to wait until Colin comes in. I didn't think you'd notice."

"Of course I'm going to notice. They're completely different. One tastes nice and the other one doesn't, and you haven't even tried to make it look like it's a pint of Estrella as you've put it in a Guiness glass. Somehow, you've managed to put the wrong beer in the wrong glass."

"Would you prefer a pint of Guinness then?"

"No, I wanted a pint of Estrella, that's why I ordered one."

"Estrella's off."

"Yeah, I know. Look I'm really sorry but I can't drink this. What other lagers do you have that are available?"

"Budweiser"

"No, I just said I really can't drink Budweiser. Other than Budweiser and Estrella what else, in the way of lager, is available for me to have?"

The woman looked around at the various taps, "Aspall?" she said.

"That's cider."

"Oh, is it? I must have meant Amstel."

"Okay, I'll have a pint of that then."

The young woman behind the bar bent down to search amongst the clean glasses and after a few minutes resurfaced with an Aspall glass.

"No, sorry, it was actually a pint of Amstel that I asked for."

"I know, I'm just getting it for you."

"It's just that you've got an Aspall glass."

"It doesn't matter, does it?"

"Well, I'd rather an Amstel glass if you've got one."

Without bothering to re-check, the young woman said, "We haven't got any."

"Alright, I suppose it doesn't really matter."

The young woman started pouring the pint of Amstel into the Aspall glass and then picked up the card machine.

"Sorry, but you aren't expecting me to pay for that, are you?"

She leapt across and abruptly turned off the Amstel tap saying, "I was told that the only thing I shouldn't charge for is tap water, even though we include ice and a slice of lemon with it."

"Yes, but you gave me a pint of Budweiser which I didn't want, instead of a pint of Estrella which I did want, and which I've already paid for. I am therefore returning the unwanted pint of Budweiser in exchange for a pint of Amstel."

"But you've already drunk some of it."

"That's because I didn't know it wasn't Estrella until I tried it."

"Okay. How about I top it up with the Amstel I've just poured and only charge you for a quarter of a pint? That way everybody's happy."

"I'm sorry, that really isn't going to work. Can't you just give me a replacement pint of Amstel?"

"No, I'm going to have to wait for Colin to come in. He should be here in about ten minutes. Can you wait until then?"

"You haven't worked in a pub before, have you?" he said in a compassionate tone.

"I beg your pardon, Mr. Cheeky Chops. What makes you say that? I worked in The Edgar Alan Poe for a couple of days before being headhunted by The Willem Defoe."

"It's Daniel."

"Hello Daniel, my name's Lucy. Colin will be in shortly. He's the manager, so he should be able to resolve this mess," said Lucy, giving him another large friendly smile.

He went back to his table and sat quietly, watching the door with his discarded pint of Budweiser still three quarters full. He was now awaiting the arrival of Colin, as well as the woman he had arranged to meet.

He had met her in The Dance Tunnel in Dalston, the previous Saturday. They had gone back to his flat, which was close by, after the club had closed at 6am, and spent the whole of Sunday morning and the best part of the afternoon drinking, snorting, laughing and talking complete nonsense. Once the alcohol and drugs had run out, around six in the evening, she'd suggested they call it a day and go to bed. By that time, they were both incapable of attempting anything more than hugging and kissing, but that had seemed just perfect. He'd had a wonderful time and couldn't wait to see her again. On this occasion they'd agreed to be sensible, as it was a Thursday, and maybe just have a few drinks before going for something to eat in one of the many restaurants near to where she lived. He'd brought a gram of coke with him though, just in case. Better to have it and not want it than to want it and not have it, he'd decided pragmatically.

The door opened and the woman he'd been waiting for walked in to the pub, her head glancing agitatedly around before finally noticing him and making her way over to where he was seated. He stood up and went to give her a kiss on the lips, and she quickly turned her head to one side, offering him her cheek.

"Hello, how are you doing?" he said

"Tired," she replied, sitting down.

"Do you mind if we go somewhere else? It's all a bit too weird in here."

"But you've hardly touched your drink. Where do you want to go?"

"It's not mine. It's a long story. I don't know. Anywhere."

"Alright, if we really have to, let's go to The Edgar Alan Poe."

"Perfect," he replied, despite never having been there before.

They both stood up and made their way to the front door. Once they were on the pavement, he went to hold her hand. "Do you mind if we don't, I'm too tired?" she said, and he decided not to say anything.

They walked in silence for the next ten minutes until they reached the replacement pub. "Let me get you a drink, hopefully that'll make you feel a lot better," he said.

"I'm alright, there's nothing wrong with me, I'm just tired that's all," she snapped back, before going off to find a table while he ordered the drinks.

Once he had placed the drinks on the table and sat down, he said as gently as he could, "Look, if you'd rather not do this tonight, we can always do it another time."

"Well, we're already here now, aren't we?"

"Yes. And it's so good to see you again. I've been really looking forward to it."

"Aw," she said, before taking a sip of her drink.

After a few minutes of painful silence, he said, "Do you want a line? It might liven you up."

"What? You've brought gear out with you? I thought we were going to go for something to eat."

"Yeah, but we don't have to do any of it, if you don't want to."

"Well, you obviously do, otherwise you wouldn't have brought it out with you."

"No, honestly, I don't. I just thought...," he left it at that, not really sure what to say and now wishing he hadn't mentioned it in the first place.

After what seemed like an even longer period of silence, she said "My ex-boyfriend had a drug problem like you. It was horrible. I didn't know where he was half the time."

"I really haven't got a drug problem. Sorry, I shouldn't have said anything."

"He couldn't get the horn either."

"What? I can always get the horn whenever I want. I've never had a problem with that. Touch wood."

"And the amount of bollocks he used to talk when I did see him. Even worse than you. I sometimes used to think I actually preferred it when he was off getting twatted with any old Tom Dick & Harry. At least I knew he wasn't having an affair."

"Alright, do you want another drink, or shall we get something to eat?"

"The cunt then fucked off with my best mate. Fucking good luck to pair of them, that's what I say. *She* can lie there with her legs open getting all pissed off while he frantically tugs on his limp dick like a lunatic for half an hour trying to get a hard on."

"I'll go and get another drink," he said.

"No, let's go and eat. I'm hungry now," she said, standing up and draining her glass.

"Do you like Keralan food?" She asked him when they were back outside.

"Yes, Indian is good," he replied.

"No, this is Keralan, it's from Kerala. I know Kerala is in India, but this place is completely different. They do a lot of fish."

"That sounds great," he said, as he began to wonder what on earth he was still doing there.

They reached 'The Jewel of South India – Home of Food from Kerala & Karnataka' which was not much further away in Stoke Newington High Street. The restaurant, like all Indian restaurants these days, looked just like any other restaurant. Indian, Keralan or otherwise. The flock wallpaper and homely booths now sadly, long gone and replaced by the generic style of white walls and steel tables.

"Are we getting starters?" she said, looking at the menu, once they were seated. "Here's something you probably haven't said you've had before: Mysore Bona."

"It's not pronounced boner, its actually Mysore Bonda. Yes, let's get one of them," he said, deciding not to react to her attempt at humiliation. "Then for the main course I'm going to have the Thiruvananthapuram Style Fish Curry," he continued, closing the menu and placing it on the table.

"I thought if you were having a fish dish, a small Kochi one would have been right up your straße," she said Germanically.

"I think the correct pronunciations is actually Ko-Chee," he replied. "I'm sure that's nice, but I'll stick with the Thiruvananthapuram. Do you know what you want?"

"I like the sound of the Poovar Beach Style Fish, but it reminds me of one of those machines they use to vacuum up those little shit-balls you get on a farm. I might just have Chicken Tikka Masala. No, tell a lie, I'm going to try the same as you. I've not had that before, but you can order it for me as you're such an expert in Keralan pronunciation."

"Alright, and I'll order some rice as well. Anything else?"

"How about a Sambar?"

"Okay, but maybe we should order the food first before we start dancing," he said, and noticed that for the first time that night she was smiling at him, and it almost melted his heart.

* * *

They both enjoyed a really excellent meal, putting all their concentration into eating rather than talking and left the restaurant feeling pleasantly fulfilled. "What do you fancy doing now?" he said, as they stood outside smoking.

"Nothing, I'm going to go home," she replied.

"Okay," he said, trying to hide his disappointment.

"You can come back if you want."

"Oh, alright. I wasn't sure. That'd be great. Thanks"

After walking the short distance back up Church Street and turning off into one of the many side roads, he couldn't help but feel that the evening was progressing a lot better than he'd anticipated earlier. Maybe she was a little nervous as well as tired, and that's why she gave the impression that she absolutely detested him. She seemed a lot more like her old self now. Well, the old self he remembered from the only time he'd previously spent with her, anyway.

She opened the door to her flat and they walked up the stairs in to her living room. He had always found it exciting when someone you were attracted to first took you back to where they lived. It meant finding out so much more about them. What their taste in furniture was like, how good their record collection was and whether the place was clean and tidy. The answers to these questions told you a lot about a person and whether or not you wanted to pursue the relationship. By far the most thrilling part though, was going in to that person's bedroom. It was undoubtedly the most intimate room in their home, and being invited in there made him somehow feel, privileged. This was where he found himself now after she'd said, "Do you mind if we go straight to bed?"

He undressed and got in to bed while she was in the bathroom. When she returned, she'd changed into a pair of grey and brown plaid brushed cotton pyjamas. Even though they looked horrible, he still found himself attracted to her. That was surely a good sign, he decided. She got in to bed and wished him good night before switching off the bedside lamp and turning over to face the opposite direction to where he was lying.

"Is it alright if I give you a hug," he whispered.

"I really am too tired," she replied.

He leant over and gave her a kiss on the back of her head and continued to lie there, silently still, for a good few hours before finally falling asleep.

They were awoken by the alarm clock. After wishing each other "Good Morning", he got out of bed and went to the bathroom. Once he'd returned, he noticed that the whole bedroom smelt strangely unpleasant. He assumed that as soon as he'd gone out of the room she must have surreptitiously broken wind, perhaps even several times, hoping that any smell would have disappeared without trace by the time he'd got back. Instead of mentioning anything, he thought it only polite to make himself scarce for a little while. So, he turned around and went back to the bathroom, pretending that he still had unfinished business to attend to.

He dressed quickly. "Right, I'm going to make a move now. Thanks for a lovely evening," he said, bending down to give her a kiss goodbye. "When shall we meet up, next?" he asked.

"Can we leave it for a bit? It feels like I've really been burning the candle at both ends and need to have a breather from going out and getting totally hammered. It's been relentless. Let's speak in a couple of weeks, I should be ready by then," she replied, as she lay there with her eyes closed.

"Okay. I'll leave it up to you. Give me a call whenever you're ready to meet up again."

"No, you give me a call in a couple of weeks."
"Okay. What time?"
"Anytime you want."
"Alright," he said, before making his way down the stairs.

As he was closing the front door behind him, he heard what sounded like a massive fart coming from the direction of the bedroom.

* * *

At least it was now Friday, he contemplated, as he walked along Stoke Newington High Street on his way back home to Dalston. It was relatively quiet at this time in the morning, and with the sun already shining in a clear blue sky, he happily let his mind run free. He had plans to go out later that night and could hardly wait for it to come round. He pictured himself walking down Kingsland High Street, just before midnight, unconcerned by the crowds of people making their way to and from the numerous restaurants and bars. That emphatic feeling, he always had, that his night was really only just beginning. He would see the gleaming neon lights of the sign for Voodoo Ray's pizza place, which was above the club, and feel his heart beat that little bit faster. He would be welcomed by the smiling, friendly security guy who stood in front of the small dark grey door, on which were black stenciled letters that excitingly, read 'Dance Tunnel.'

He would make his way down the spiral staircase and at once be embraced by the wonderful, irresistible, sound of House Music. His name would be checked against the ticket list, and he'd have his wrist stamped in black ink with the words, 'Tunnel Dancer'. Pushing open the double doors, the music would be much louder now, and he would feel the intensity and energy emanating from those people already dancing inside. The cloakroom was directly to his left and the bar to his right and the rest was the dance floor. Somebody had once said to him that they didn't like the club because 'there was nowhere to go.' That was exactly why he did like it. He'd get himself a drink and have a brief chat with anybody he recognized; people who, despite only ever seeing him here, would hug and accept him as a close friend. People of various nationalities, different races, contrasting sexual preferences, but all with the same intentions: to dance away the pain and misery of their lives in a hot, dark, sweaty, smoke-filled basement with one red light; and feel like they were part of a utopian society of 200 like-minded souls if only for six hours. A society where hateful, ignorant, selfish and uncompassionate people did not exist. He'd decided long ago that going to a club, taking drugs and dancing all night was the one place where he felt completely comfortable and the only time he truly liked himself.

    Then on Saturday, he thought, he might go back to that pub again and see if Lucy the barmaid was in there. He was sure she fancied him. The proof would be if she remembered his name.

1940

Harry was sitting upstairs on the number 73 bus smoking a cigarette. He had a smug smile on his face and still couldn't quite believe that he'd managed to wangle leave from the training camp for a whole Saturday night. Three months of marching, loading rifles, physical exercise and learning the best way to stick a bayonet in somebody's body or cut their throat with a knife had demoralised him, and he was now looking forward to having a few pints in the pub and seeing Doris again.

Bloody war, thought Harry, it was nearly December and wasn't it all supposed to have been over by Christmas, or was that last Christmas? Perhaps he was getting confused with the last war. Anyhow, another month and he would have finished his training and then, according to the regulations, inevitably have to join some corps or other. Get posted overseas and be expected to fight against men he'd never met, who came from countries he'd never been to. There was no sign of this whole mess finishing any time soon, so he was going to make the most of his night of freedom.

It'd been a stroke of luck chatting to that feller, Joe. What was it he'd called the Seargeant Major again? That's right, a misogynist, Harry remembered after racking his brains. Bit of a smart alec that Joe, thinks he's a cut above everybody else. Anyway, when he'd mentioned to Joe that he would do anything to get away from the barracks for a day, Joe told him that could easily be sorted out.

"Just go and see the Seargeant Major. Pretend that you suspect your other half is carrying on," Joe had said. "The bloke's a proper misogynist, I've heard. If he thinks you're going to knock her about a bit, he's more than willing to let you have a little bit of extracurricular combat training."

Harry had to ask know-it-all Joe what extracurricular meant as well, but credit where credit's due, he'd been right and the Seargeant Major didn't hesitate to let him take some compassionate leave.

"You go and sort her out, good and proper. Show her who's boss. And you make sure she doesn't do something like that to you again in a hurry," the Seargeant Major had said, with a look on his face that would've made Harry shudder if he hadn't been trying so hard to contain his excitement at being free for the best part of the forthcoming weekend.

Everybody else on the bus looked miserable Harry noticed as he looked around. A lot more than he seemed to remember them looking three months ago, prior to him getting called up and dragged off to somewhere he could only ever have imagined going to in his wildest dreams, Bedfordshire.

An older woman, who was sitting opposite Harry in the bus, seemed to be staring at him, he noticed. Unable to suppress his curiosity, Harry asked, "Can I help you Missus?"

"Eh?" said the woman, somewhat startled that her nosiness had been recognized.

"You were looking at me," smiled Harry. "I just wondered why you couldn't keep your peepers off me, that's all."

"Well, if you must know, young man, I wondered why you had that bloody stupid grin on your face. You do know there's a war on, I suppose?"

"I did hear something about it, yes. Probably when they told me I've got to go off and fight in it next month."

"Well, what've you got to smile about then?"

"Because, Missus, I have been let out of the barracks to go home and enjoy this beautiful October night, right the way through until Sunday evening."

"So, they're giving soldiers the weekend off now, are they? I've heard it all now. I suppose the bloody Germans all take the weekend off as well, do they? That's why there's no need for you to protect us at the weekends anymore, and you can all bugger off home and enjoy yourselves."

"Look Missus, I'd love to sit and talk with you all night but this here's my stop, so I'll say goodbye. Have a good evening."

"A good evening? Oh yes, I can't wait, Sonny. What time are they dropping the bombs on us tonight, then? You're in the army, you should know. Why can't you be useful and tell people that? Instead of just sitting there, smiling away like some gormless, Cheshire cat."

If she's anything to go by, people definitely seem to have got grumpier and a lot more stupid over the past three months, Harry concluded, as he got off the bus at Stoke Newington Common. He'd already decided that he wasn't going to let some doolally, stroppy, old biddy ruin his leave, and was determined to enjoy what might be his last time at home for, well, who knows when? He didn't want to even think about that.

Harry looked at his watch and saw that it was half past six already. Doris is going to get a big surprise when she sees me, he thought, smiling to himself. I'm sure she's missed me as much as I've missed her. As he passed the small parade of shops just opposite the road in which he lived, he decided to pick up a few bottles of beer from Jack's Off Licence to take home. Might as well celebrate and get the night started straight away.

He walked down his unlit road, having to use his torch for assistance. As he reached his front door there was a feeling of trepidation, as well as excitement, as he inserted his key into the lock. Harry's mood quickly turned to disappointment when he discovered that the flat was in complete darkness, and there was no sign of Doris, at all.

After turning on the lights, and checking the all the rooms, he decided to unnecessarily seek clarification.

"Doris? Are you home? It's me, Harry."

When, unsurprisingly, there was no response, he felt completely stupid for enquiring. Sometimes, despair caused by the unexpected makes people do irrational things. This certainly wasn't how he'd envisaged his triumphant homecoming. Not wanting to stay in an empty flat and drink beer on his own, Harry decided to go straight back out. Maybe Doris was in their local pub, he considered. Either way, he could go and have a pint there anyway. He shouldn't really be disheartened that Doris wasn't home, he now tried to convince himself. It wasn't like she was expecting him or anything. So, he endeavored to shake off his despondency in the short time it took him to walk up to The Cockhanger's Arms - so called in deference to the original name of Stoke Newington Common.

As Harry opened the door to the Public Bar, he was at once embraced by the warm comforting atmosphere of a smokey pub on a cold dark night. It wasn't too crowded at this time and looking around he couldn't see any sign of Doris. Harry made his way to the bar and ordered the pint he'd been looking forward to all day. It tasted really good, but he was certain it would have tasted all the better if Doris had been with him, or if he even knew where she was.

"Wotcher Harry. Long time, no see. What the bloody hell are you doing in here?"

Harry turned round and saw Jim, the pub landlord. "Alright, Jim? You haven't seen my Doris tonight, have you? I'm back for the weekend and thought I'd give her a nice surprise."

"Erm, yes, I have. I think you just missed her; she was in the Lounge Bar a little while ago."

"Really? That's not like her to pay more for her drinks. Who was she in there with?"

"Oh, I'm not sure. Just one of her friends, I suppose."

"You don't know where she was going, do you?"

"No, sorry Harry. I didn't speak to her."

Harry finished the rest of his pint and placed the empty glass on the bar. "Alright, thanks Jim, she's probably gone home. I'll see you around."

"Don't rush off yet, Harry. Have another drink. On the house."

"No, I'd better get back home, see if she is there. If she's not, I'll come back and take you up on that offer. She wasn't expecting me you see, so she might have made other plans."

"Alright Harry, I understand. You look after yourself and don't go doing anything I wouldn't do."

"What, like go and fight in a war, you mean?"

"You know what I'm talking about. Don't do anything stupid."

Harry walked out of the pub and back into the cold night air. He was soon back at the flat and before he'd even opened the front door, Harry sensed he was all alone. He didn't bother calling out Doris' name this time. Instead, he turned on the light, took off his coat and sat down at the desolate table. Hopefully, Doris will be back soon, Harry thought. At one point he contemplated going back to the pub but decided against it. After a further hour,

Harry's boredom was turning to anxiety. He thought about going out again, maybe to a different pub, but then he dismissed that idea as well as he wasn't really in the mood. He also didn't want to miss Doris when she did come back. So, he decided to stay where he was, all by himself, drinking the beer he'd bought to celebrate his immorally acquired leave.

Two hours later there was still no sign of Doris. Harry had finished all the bottles of beer and was now walking up and down the small living room, in an agitated state, with only his deep inner thoughts for company. I'd have been better off staying where I was, instead of being stuck here all on my own. I wish I'd been able to warn her I was coming home. She wasn't to know, was she? It's not her fault she has gone out for a drink with one of her friends. I really wish she would walk in the door right this minute, I can't wait to see her again.

Harry's reverie was interrupted by the haunting sound of an air raid siren. He pulled back the heavy curtains a fraction and looked up at the night sky. Beams of light in all directions illuminated the darkness, and people in the street were running towards their nearest shelter. Harry decided to stay where he was. The last time he'd been in one of those shelters it'd been awful. People singing, snoring or stinking the place out with their farting, while all the time you were worrying if your house was still going to be there when you finally got out the following morning. Fuck it! I'll stay here and take my chances, he decided. Doris might come home now as well, he hoped. She hated those shelters as much as he did. He turned off the light just in case one of those interfering ARP Wardens suspected he was still in there. He then put on his regulation tin hat and sat under the kitchen table waiting for the all-clear.

An hour and a half later, Harry heard the eerie single continuous note of the siren indicating that the air raid was over for now. He crawled out from under the kitchen table, took off his tin hat and began pacing up and down the living room again. This was worse than being in the barracks, he thought, and a lot more dangerous. Perhaps Doris had decided to go to a shelter after all and might not be home now until the morning. There was no way he could go to bed; he wouldn't be able to sleep. He decided he would sit up and wait for Doris to come home safely, hoping more than anything else that this would be sooner rather than later, and then they could get into a nice warm comfortable bed together. He couldn't wait to hold her in his arms.

Harry must have dropped off to sleep at some point, and when he awoke, he was not entirely sure at first where he was. The coal fire had burnt itself out and he felt cold and lonely. As soon as he'd got his bearings, his thoughts once again turned to Doris. If she wasn't home in the next couple of hours, he didn't know what he would do. He got up from his chair and walked towards the window. Looking out, he could see that everywhere was deathly quiet and there was a murky, uninviting greyness which made Harry want to stay exactly where he was. There didn't appear to be any buildings near him that had been bombed, which was surprising. Last night, it had felt as if everywhere around him was taking the full force of the Luftwaffe's bombs, and it was only a matter of time before one landed on his kitchen table. He just hoped that Doris, wherever she was, had been as lucky. Harry began pacing up and down his living room once again, still not certain about what he should do next. Perhaps he should go out and ask around to see if anybody knew where Doris had gone last night, but he was now too frightened of what he might find out. Harry therefore decided to stay put. At least, that way, he would be there when she did come back.

The hours wore painfully on, and the specified time that Harry should have returned to the barracks had long passed. He'd decided that there was no way he could leave home until he was certain that Doris was safe. Although he'd been given strict instructions not to exceed his twenty-four-hour leave, surely, they would understand why he couldn't return to the camp. It was crucial that he saw Doris again, and more important to him than anything on earth.

He sat reminiscing about the last time he'd seen Doris. They'd got drunk together and stayed up all through the hot July night, talking. He'd told her how much he loved her, how lucky he was to have somebody he felt so close to and that he couldn't stand the thought of leaving her. How scared he was that he might never see her again. He'd then been overcome by an extraordinary wave of passion and had dragged Doris to the floor. He lifted her skirt up over her waist and had frenziedly pulled down her knickers. The excitement he'd felt was incredible, and he just managed to get his trousers and underpants down, before ejaculating all over Doris's recently exposed mons pubis. That's what clever clogs Joe had said it was called, anyway. He apologized uneasily, as Doris silently lay there with her eyes closed and tears streaming down her beautiful face. After quickly rearranging his trousers and underpants, he'd then put on his jacket and hat, picked up his suitcase and walked trance-like out of the front door.

Harry was surprised that replaying this scene in his mind had caused him to become extremely aroused. He walked towards Doris's chest of drawers, opened the top one and took out a pair of knickers. He gently pressed them against his face, then ran his fingers slowly through them, doing the same with one of her brassieres and a pair of her stockings he'd found in the next drawer down. Harry began to quickly undress. He had a yearning to be as close to Doris as was humanly possible at that particular moment. Harry placed his left foot into one of the stockings, slowly rolling it up his leg towards his thigh, and did the same with his right foot. He was then able to securely attach both stockings to the suspender belt he'd handily come upon when his fingers excitedly probed Doris's bottom drawer. Harry carefully put on the brassiere, leaving the knickers until last, as he knew these would excite him the most. Then, hands on hips, Harry admired himself in the mirror and felt a phenomenal surge of lust which he somehow, was able to resist, albeit with considerable difficulty. Harry wanted to see how long he could prolong this emotional state before temptation would, inevitably, overcome him.

Just as he was contemplating making himself a cup of tea and a strawberry jam sandwich, there was a loud banging on his front door. Harry's first reaction was to simply ignore it. Hopefully, whoever it was would go away. Then, just as he was thinking that it might be important and have something to do with Doris, the banging started again.

"Who is it?" Harry asked, as calmly as anybody could possibly be expected to, when dressed only in unfamiliar underwear belonging to a person of the opposite sex.

"Police. Open up."

"Just a minute," Harry replied, somewhat less composed and clearly no longer aroused. As the banging on the door increased, Harry ran around in a panic looking for his clothes.

"Open this door, now."

When Harry didn't answer because he was too busy trying to put on his trousers and shirt over Doris's underwear, he heard more furious banging.

"If you don't open this fucking door right now, we're going to knock it down."

Shit, it must be the Redcaps, thought Harry. The police don't usually threaten to smash your door down if they've come to give you news about somebody. Even if they think it happens to be extremely good news. The sort of news that he'd been hoping for, and desperately wanted to hear more than anything else in the whole world. The news that Doris, his lovely twin sister, was thankfully safe and sound, after all.

7 O'Clock Drop

It was almost two thirty and a light May drizzle was starting to fall as they came out of the all-night off licence. All five of them were carrying blue plastic bags, filled with assorted bottles and cans of alcohol. Luckily, somebody had also remembered to get cigarettes.

"So, this place is open all night, is it?" asked Godfrey.

"Yeah, that's why it's called The All-Night Off Licence," replied Albert, who was the designated after party host for the night, seeing that he lived closest to The Drop, a small basement club beneath The Three Crowns Pub on the corner of Stoke Newington Church Street. They'd had a great time at a brand-new club night called A Love From Outer Space.

"That's useful," said Walter. "We're not going to run out of refreshments then."

"Yeah, but we don't want to have to keep coming down here though, do we?" Albert said. "Are we sure we've got everything?" he asked.

"I should coco," Vera replied. "It is only a Thursday night, after all. Some of us have got to pretend they're actually doing something while they're supposed to be working from home tomorrow, and not just sitting in their pants watching Cash in the Attic."

"Well, some of us have got to phone in sick by nine," said Dolly. "I can probably only stay until about eight. That's eight, tomorrow evening, by the way," she laughed, before loudly singing a vocal line from one of the tracks that had been played earlier in the club.

"Keep the noise down," whispered Albert, as they walked down the deserted residential street. "We don't want anyone to call the police."

"That's right. They'll be droves of them over here in a shot as they've probably got fuck all else to do at this time of night," Walter concurred.

"Exactly, so just be quiet for a little bit longer. We'll be there soon," Albert said, while making his way to the front of the procession to lead them on the final straight home, like five astronauts returning to the safety of the space station after a successful mission.

Once they were all back at Albert's flat, they began the process of making themselves comfortable. Albert and Vera were in the kitchen mixing drinks, Godfrey was sat on the floor racking up lines of coke on a large mirror and Dolly was dancing with Walter and singing along to the music, irrespective of whether the track had any vocals or not.

"I wish I lived in a new build like this, and my flat was soundproofed," Vera said to Albert. "Where I live, I've had neighbours directly north, south, east & west of me complaining about the noise. Usually, all at the same time."

"I worry sometimes though, that maybe it isn't as well soundproofed as I think it is," Albert said, getting the ice out of the freezer. "I've got visions of my doorbell being rung one day, and when I open the door, all twenty residents from the other flats in this block are going to be standing there in their dressing gowns, telling me to turn it down."

"If that was going to happen, I'm sure it would have happened by now, considering some of the parties you've had round here. Or maybe you've just got much nicer neighbours who are a lot more understanding than the ones I've got," said Vera, laughing a little louder than she normally would in her own home at 3 a.m.

Albert and Vera then made their way into the living room to join the others, and get the party properly started.

* * *

After three hours had flown by, everybody was still having a marvellous time. Drinking, smoking, snorting, dancing, chatting complete nonsense and laughing. Nobody had a care in the world and if they did, not one they would care to remember.

"Do you think you'll ever get bored of doing this?" said Walter to nobody in particular.

"No way. How long have we all been doing this now? Since 1986. So that's what, twenty-four years. Nearly a quarter of a century, and they still haven't invented a better way to spend a night. Or a morning or an afternoon, come to that." Albert replied.

"I totally agree, but I got a bit freaked out the other day thinking about still going to clubs at our age. I know it isn't just us and there were loads of people there tonight even older than we are, but when my dad was my age, I was in my early twenties. If my dad had told me then that he was going out to a club, I would have been fucking mortified," said Vera.

"Yeah, but don't you ever think we are only still doing this because we are just chasing that first buzz we got from the whole Acid House scene?" said Walter. "Once we'd got involved, we were addicted straight away and then we're always chasing that initial feeling, just like a junky does."

7 O'Clock Drop

"We're not junkies," said Dolly. "We're totally in control."

At that moment Godfrey, who had been very quiet for the last hour, passed out, hitting his head on the side of Albert's occasional table.

"Shit! He almost knocked over the rest of the gear," Albert exclaimed, rushing over to secure the contents.

"Is he alright?" asked Vera

"He's not dead, is he?" laughed Dolly.

Vera went over to attend to Godfrey, who was lying motionless on the living room floor. After turning him over and calling his name several times, there was still no response. "Has anybody got a mirror?" she asked.

"Now isn't the time to be checking your hair and make-up," Dolly said, still laughing.

"I want to see if he's breathing," replied Vera.

"There's only that big one on the table and that's got what's left of all the gear on it," said Albert.

Luckily, before any crucial, matter of life-or-death decisions had to be made, Godfrey opened one eye briefly before slowly closing it again.

"Don't worry, I think he's alright," Vera said, before taking a deep breath and slowly exhaling.

"He's probably just tired, let him sleep," said Walter, lifting the mirror and putting it in a safe place, much closer to where he was sitting. "What would we have done if he *was* dead?"

"We'd have had to carry him to the police station and then just left him outside," Albert declared, in a tone which implied that the answer was obvious.

"You mean the hospital, don't you?" enquired Vera.

"No, the police station. It's a lot nearer. It's only over the road. The hospital's miles away and if he's already dead, what can the hospital do about it, anyway?"

"You are joking, aren't you?" asked Vera, with a concerned look which involved raising one eyebrow.

"Of course I am," Albert answered, walking off to get himself another drink.

Despite nobody carrying out any further examinations on him, his four friends diagnosed Godfrey's near-death experience to possibly be a result of him getting up too early for work that morning, not eating properly before going out, still being upset about the breakup of his marriage twenty-two years ago (which also coincided with the mysterious death of his dog shortly afterwards), too much booze or those last two pills he decided to crush up and snort in one go. They eventually agreed that it was most likely a combination of all of these, although a similar thing had happened last Sunday morning as well, they seemed to remember. While Godfrey continued to sleep like a baby, albeit one that had consumed copious amounts of booze and drugs, the remaining four decided to carry on with their activities.

* * *

Another hour passed by in no time at all. The pale sunlight, which had crept into the room like an unwanted trespasser, began to make everybody feel uneasy. The music was turned down a little, and even Dolly was no longer singing and dancing. The mirror was still being passed around amongst the seated group and, despite becoming noticeably more subdued, the conversation continued to flow like diverted flood waters from an intentionally exploded levee.

"Do you remember some of those really early Acid House nights we used to go to?" Walter asked, deciding to help himself to another line from the mirror next to him.

"Of course, how could we ever forget. At that moment in our lives, it was probably the most exciting thing we had ever experienced," Albert replied. "It blew our heads off."

"It still is the most exciting thing. And how good were the pills back then," Walter proclaimed.

"We were totally off our tits." said Dolly.

"And they lasted all night, whatever you did," Vera added.

"That's right," said Dolly. "Even if you had to go for a disco shit."

"What the fuck is a disco shit?" laughed Albert.

"You know," Dolly replied. "When you start coming up on a pill and you get a really strong rush and then you have to go for a Forest Gump."

"So, why isn't it called a disco dump instead then?" asked Walter.

"Because people already use that to describe that club up in Manchester," said Albert, unable to remember the name of the place he was thinking of.

"Isn't a disco shit like a disco nap? asked Vera. "Which is what you have *before* you go out. So that must be what it's called when you were so excited about going out that night, that you had to go to the toilet?"

"No, that's just called going for a shit," laughed Albert, before standing up. "Talking of which..."

"Enjoy your after-party shit," said Walter. "That reminds me, I did this massive shit the other day. It was like giving birth. It was such hard work trying to get it out, that by the end of it I was sweating like a dinner lady and had taken all my clothes off, including my shoes and socks."

"Can we please stop talking shit?" said Vera, reaching over to the contents on the mirror again.

"If anyone is in need of a rest and wants to go to the rest room, I'd give it 10 minutes if I were you," Albert announced, returning from the toilet sometime later.

Dolly and Vera were too busy talking to each other to take any notice and Albert walked over to where Walter was sitting and said, "I was just thinking, do you remember that time we were all supposed to go on that beano down to Margate for the Boy's Own party, and the coach never turned up?"

"I remember going to Margate, but I don't remember the coach not turning up. How did we get there then?" Walter asked.

"You had to drive," Albert replied.

"I don't remember that. Are you sure?"

"Absolutely. I remember it as clearly as if it was yesterday, even though it was, what? Around twenty-three years ago. There was an all dayer followed by an all nighter, or was it the other way round, and for some reason we all met in that poncey wine bar near Clapton Pond. The one that got mysteriously burnt down and isn't there anymore. What was it called?"

"The Old Fire Station."

"That's it. So, you do remember it."

"I remember us all going to Margate and having a great time, and isn't that when Godfrey shat himself on the way home? But I definitely don't remember driving."

"That's weird that you can remember that, but you can't recall driving. Hey, Vera, Dolly, do you remember us all going to Margate back in 1987?"

"Is that when Godfrey shat himself at the traffic lights?" asked Dolly.

"Yes!" Albert & Walter said, in unison.

"That's the only bit I remember," laughed Dolly.

"Yeah, I remember it," Vera said. "We had a brilliant time."

"Do you remember how we got there, though?" asked Walter.

"Wasn't that when we were all a bit trolleyed in some pub and Albert had to drive for some reason," Vera replied.

"No! I drove," exclaimed Walter. "Well, according to Albert I did, anyway. The coach never turned up."

"How strange is that, eh?" said Albert. "All of us were there together, and we are all certain of some things that definitely happened, but some of us can't remember other things that happened while some of us can."

"We must have forgotten," said Walter.

"Eh? How can you forget you drove to Margate and back again? asked Albert. "And why did you forget that bit but still remember all the other stuff? It must be selective memory. Maybe you've chosen to forget it subconsciously because it was a traumatic experience. And what's suddenly made me think of it again? I haven't thought about it for years."

"Maybe you thought of Godfrey in Margate because you were in the toilet," laughed Dolly.

"I don't think of Godfrey or Margate every time I go to the toilet. No, there's more to it than that," replied Albert, looking in turn at each member of his captive audience, before continuing, "I reckon the brain remembers every single thing that's happened in our lives but we either don't know how to recall all of that information or somehow, it gets buried in the back of our minds. So, sometimes we just need a catalyst to trigger off a memory which seems to come out of nowhere. Everyone's had an experience like that before, haven't they?"

"I know what you mean," said Walter. "Every time I smell chlorine it takes me back to swimming lessons at these school baths we had to go to when I was about eleven. It happened again when I opened that last wrap of coke. I hated the instructor as he was always picking on me. It came out later that the horrible little fucker was part of some paedophile ring. Apparently, there were a load of them working in swimming baths all over the country, and they used to secretly photograph all the kids in the changing rooms and exchange pictures."

"That's right, I remember the headline in The Guardian when it came out, it was Paedos in Speedos," laughed Dolly.

"Yeah, and The Independent's was Speedo-Philes," Albert added.

"It's not funny. I thought we were having a serious conversation," Walter said, helping himself to another line of coke before sitting back down, silently lost in thought.

"I get it all the time with smells, as well," said Vera. "Freshly cut grass on a hot day, the smell of the first day of spring or a freezing cold winter's day when the sky is blue, and the sun is shining. It always takes me back to an exact same feeling I had on a day just like that, sometime in the past. Then I remember something that I hadn't thought about in years."

"I saw an advert the other day for this record that's coming out, and it's on coloured vinyl, but in these really weird colours divided into three blocks, red, lime green and orange," said Albert. "I immediately got a flashback of an ice lolly I used to like when I was a little kid. I probably haven't thought about that ice lolly for about forty years."

"This reminds me of a story my sister told me the other day," said Vera. "You know she's a special needs teacher, right? Well, she's been working with these extremely severe cases who have all got really excessive disabilities."

"What, they've got wheelchairs and mobility scooters?" asked Dolly.

"No, not physical. Mental disabilities," Vera replied. "Anyway, she said they're all such sweet kids and she absolutely loves working with them. Some of them are a more responsive than others, so she always gets mixed results when she tries something in a lesson. One of the things she was doing was showing different objects and asking them to name what each one was. There's this one kid, and whatever object she showed them, he would always shout out the same thing every time - 'Hamburger.'"

"What's his name, Ronald McDonald?" enquired Dolly.

"No, it's Casey Jones," laughed Albert, before asking in a slightly more serious tone, "And it wasn't a hamburger, at all?"

"No, nothing like it."

"What did your sister say? Dolly asked, 'It's a good guess, but it's not the right answer' like that Roy Walker fella off of Catchphrase." Before adding, "Say what you see," in a soft Northern Irish accent.

"I doubt it. You know what she's like, she's lovely. She just carried on. Probably tried to give him a clue to help him."

"Why did he keep saying 'Hamburger,' was that his favourite food, then?" Albert asked.

"It is now," Dolly laughed. "What would you like for breakfast, lunch and dinner, Ronald? - Hamburger."

"I'm not sure that anybody asks him what he specifically wants to eat now. The poor kid lives in the residential part of the school, as his parents couldn't cope with looking after him."

"Probably sick of cooking fucking hamburgers every day," said Dolly.

"No, it's a really sad story," continued Vera, ignoring the stifled giggling sounds coming from Albert and Dolly. "About nine years ago, when he was three, his parents had another child, a little girl, despite the doctors warning them that there was a strong possibility that the daughter would also be born with similar disabilities to their son. But they went ahead with it after all, because they adored their son, despite all the extra attention he needed from them. I don't know the ins and outs of it all, but when the daughter was eighteen months old or something, she died. As you can imagine, the parents were distraught. They ended up separating and neither one of them could cope properly with looking after their son who was becoming much more demanding now, so he had to move in to the residential home at the special needs school."

"Can't we talk about something else?" said Walter, now out of his reverie. "There must be some other stories about Godfrey being spasticated we can laugh about."

"Probably not the most appropriate turn of phrase to use," said Vera, slowly shaking her head. "Anyway, I haven't quite finished the story yet. I'll be quick, and then we can get back to talking bollocks again. So, my sister is trying another lesson, but this time, rather than showing them objects, she is letting them feel them. She tries a whole load of stuff, and each time, whatever it is, this kid shouts out 'Hamburger'. Then she lets him feel this fern leaf she's brought in and waits for the inevitable response. Straight away, he looks up and gives her this great big smile and says, 'Baby sister hair.'"

The morning sunlight was now penetrating the hushed living room. Albert decides to finally break the silence. "Let's finish the last of this bugle. Who wants another nose up?" he said, holding the mirror aloft.

"One more for the road, then I'm off," said Walter, finishing his drink.

"Yeah, I'm going to make a move too," announced Dolly. "I want to give my son a call before he goes off to work. Just to say hello and check he's alright and tell him I'm thinking of him and that I love him."

"Maybe you should wait until this evening, he's bound to guess you're a bit twatted," Vera said.

"I might be a little bit wankered, but I'm definitely not twatted," Dolly replied. "Maybe you're right, though. I'll text him later, instead. Let's wake Godfrey up, I'm sure he has to be at work in a little while. He doesn't know what he's missed."

Recapture The Thrill

I don't know if anybody else remembers exactly where they were and what they did on the evening of Friday 29th September 1967, but I do. In fact, not a single day has passed since then when I haven't thought about it. My head tells me I shouldn't, but today, once again, my heart has won the argument. Perhaps, if I write it all down, I will finally get it out of my system. I seriously have my doubts that this will work but I've tried a number of other things, all to no avail, so what have I got to lose? Maybe an hour or two of my life, but when you're in your late-seventies, time, as precious as it has now become, is also, oddly, something that I have in abundance.

That year had been a memorable one for me already. Back in the summer, I had moved into an attic floor bedsit which was just by Clissold Park. When I sat staring out of the window, which I frequently did, I could see the reservoir on one side of Green Lanes, and on the other side I could just make out the mysterious looking medieval style castle building. I discovered that this was built back in Victorian times to appease the dissenting residents. They apparently didn't want an unsightly industrial reservoir pumping station spoiling the beauty of the area, so the New River Company offered to build them a much more appealing alternative to disguise the building's true purpose instead. How times have changed, eh? I'm so glad that they built a castle. This gave the area a magical feeling, or it certainly did to me - an impressionable twenty-three-year-old, who was not long down from the suburbs. I was working in an office as a clerk and earning relatively good money, enough to help satisfy my main passion which was music. There seemed to be an incredible explosion of music everywhere and it was hard to keep up with it sometimes. Every club I went to had another group playing who would, as people used to say in those days, blow my mind. I became addicted and would go out every weekend to see groups play. Perhaps even once or twice during the week as well, depending on how much money I had left to last me until pay day the following Friday.

That night I was going to The Manor House, which often had groups playing. It had become my favourite venue. As it was only a fifteen-minute walk away along Green Lanes, it was further proof, if I needed it, that I had definitely chosen the right area in which to live. The Manor House was not as grand as it sounds. It was a basic large pub downstairs, with a decent sized room upstairs where the live acts performed. There was a sign that said it had been rebuilt in 1931, but there had been a pub on that site since the 1830's. That's over a quarter of a century longer than the medieval castle and almost sixty years before Clissold Park itself. It was such a landmark that they even named the tube station after it. Whenever I told people who weren't familiar with the area that I lived in Manor House, presuming that they would have at least seen the station on the tube map, this always caused some raised eyebrows, and their first instinct was to assume that I was quite posh. I've never stayed in a real manor house, but I doubt that there's only one toilet between fifteen people, and, if there was, I imagine it would be a lot cleaner and not stink anywhere near as bad as the one in the place where I lived.

On entering the venue, I always got a twinge of excitement. I bought my ticket (which I still have from that night) and went into the room upstairs. The first thing I saw was the stage, and the reassuring sight of a drumkit, guitars, keyboard, microphones and amps, all set up and waiting patiently for somebody to transform these inanimate objects into pulsating life. I would think about the other groups I had seen here and imagine those I had missed from a time before I even knew about this place. Someone had told me that The Rolling Stones played a residency here, before they became famous, and proudly declared that it was the first venue they'd played outside of their usual haunts in the Richmond area. Hearing this made me equally proud. Can you imagine? The Stones, who went on to become the greatest, longest lasting R'n'B combo, playing just up the road from where I live. Not everyone I've told this to seemed to share the same enthusiasm though, and I've told a lot of people, believe you me.

    I made my way to the bar and ordered a bottle of Double Diamond. Not because I had been instructed by the adverts that it was, 'The beer that men drink' or 'That it works wonders, so drink one today', but because it was the only beer they had which was available in bottles. I always avoided draught beer as everyone said it was watered down by greedy landlords, especially so at The Manor House. Also, draught beer always seemed to have the effect of bloating me out and making me want to break wind, neither of which was particularly conducive to dancing to psychedelic music. I poured my beer into a glass and went to find a suitable position within the now sizable crowd. It would probably be a quarter of an hour or so before the group came on stage and that initial twinge of excitement had now risen to a tremor. I looked around with the sole purpose of killing time and noticed a woman looking in my direction who appeared to be smiling at me. To make certain it was me she was smiling at, I looked around to see who was behind me. When I saw that there was nobody smiling back at her,

I turned back and returned the smile. I now noticed that she was laughing. I started laughing as well, to give the impression that I had done that on purpose for a joke, and she started to walk over to where I was standing.

As she got closer, I could make out how beautiful she really was. It was a natural beauty that would only have been spoiled by make-up. She had long straight brown hair which went down to just below her shoulders and she was stylishly dressed in a white, long sleeve top with brown, hipster trousers and brown boots, all of which accentuated her gorgeous body.

"Hi, I'm Suzy," she said in an American accent, smiling and showing her perfectly white teeth.

"Hi" I said and told her my name.

"Where are you from?" she asked.

"Just down the road, what about you?" I replied.

"What now or originally?"

"Both"

"Okay, well originally I'm from Boring, Oregon, and now I live just down the road too."

"That's great."

"What is and why?"

"Um, you know, that you got out of somewhere dull and not very interesting and came over here."

"No, silly. The name of the place is called Boring. It's near Portland. It's named after William Boring who built a farm in the area. You guys over here might not have heard of him. But I've been living in San Francisco all year and now I'm over here in London, England."

"San Francisco? Really? Wow! I've read so much about it. What's it like?"

"It used to be really hip and was such a cool place to hang out. But it really sucks big time now. I had to get out of there pronto. Too many out of towners moving in and ruining the whole vibe."

"Oh no, that's a real shame. There's a fantastic music scene going on over there as well, isn't there?"

"Yeah, absolutely. I saw a whole bunch of great groups at the Fillmore, the Avalon and the Matrix. I couldn't stand it there any longer though. I was getting totally bummed every day. Especially when The Gray Line company started doing tours to the Haight. Can you believe they called them the Hippie Hop? Fucking buses full of people, man, driving around Haight/Ashbury, and all these fucking squares in the bus taking photographs of us. I felt like I was in some fucking goddam zoo. Those mother-fucking, shit-kicking, jerk-off, ass-wipes got me so pissed. But hey, now I'm seeing a whole shitload of great English groups over here. So, it's all good."

"I love the way you talk," I said.

"I really love your accent, too," said Suzy.

We were interrupted by a man making an announcement from the stage. "Okay, people. The time is now for a group who really are too much. Please welcome, Dantalian's Chariot."

Four men dressed entirely in white walked on to the stage and made their way to their respective instruments, which had all been painted white along with the amps. A psychedelic light show, made from a combination of oil and food colouring, was beautifully projected on to the stage and the wall behind. All four musicians were immersed in a swirl of strangely amazing patterns. They started to play their first number, 'Gemini' and the audience were at once unified by the wonderful power of music. A few songs into the set, during 'Recapture The Thrill', Suzy looked at me and gave me the most marvellous smile anybody has ever given me, either before or since. As I felt my stomach and heart churning around inside my body, I just knew that this was the start of something that would last an incredibly long time, and whatever happened from now onwards, this would be a moment I would never forget for the rest of my life.

After the last number of the set, the terrific 'Madman Running Through The Fields' had finished, and Dantalian's Chariot had left the stage, Suzy and I went to the bar to get a drink.

"Wow! That was out of sight. That totally blew my mind," she said.

"It was great, wasn't it? I can't wait to see them again. I'm going to have to check to see where and when they're playing next," I said, as I poured us both a Double Diamond.

"Do you know anything about these guys?" Suzy asked.

"Well, all I know really is that the main vocalist is a guy called Zoot Money, and he used to have an R'n'B group, and the blonde guy on guitar, who he writes a lot of the songs with, is called Andy Somers."

"Wow, man. Zoot Money. That's such a groovy name. What a great voice as well. And the bass player looks amazing. He's so tall."

"Yeah, he could have been a policeman," I said, in an attempt to make Suzy smile again.

"A pig? No fucking way, man. All four of them are way too cool to ever be in the police, especially the cute blonde guy on guitar."

Suzy must have noticed the expression on my face drastically change as I felt the stab of jealousy in my heart. She then kindly said, "Yeah, he's almost as cute as you," before giving me another one of those unforgettable smiles. "That's such a far-out name, as well. Dantalian's Chariot. Wow! Do you know where that comes from?" she continued.

"No, I don't actually, but our generation is so lucky as we have all the information we require readily available to us. All I have to do is go to the library first thing on Monday morning when they reopen, look it up and then telephone you with the answer."

"I haven't got a telephone."

"Alright, I'll write to you then. As soon as I find out the answer I'll post it to you on Monday morning, and you should know by Wednesday afternoon, at the latest."

"Ah, that's really sweet of you, but maybe you can just tell me the next time you see me."

"That'd be even better. Though thinking about it, I might not be able to get to the library until Monday lunchtime now, as I've got to be in work for nine o'clock on Monday morning."

Suzy laughed and reached out to hold my hand. She then gave me a soft, gentle kiss on the lips which made my entire body tingle from the top of my head right down to the end of my toes. We continued to hold hands as we stood drinking our beer. Maybe it really does 'work wonders' I thought, as I had truly never felt the way I was feeling at that moment. What I didn't know, or even begin to imagine, was that I would never experience a feeling like that ever again.

"You're a really funny guy. You make me laugh so much. And I really do think you're cute."

"I think you're absolutely lovely. I feel so lucky to have met you."

"Thank you, I've had such a fun night. I need to split now, though."

"Oh no. Why? Can't we do something else? It is Friday night, after all."

"We will meet again. I'm sure of it."

"When?"

"Let's leave it to fate, yeah? That's what we did all the time in the Haight. We just knew that when we met somebody, someone who we really connected with, that we would be destined to meet again. If it's meant to be, it's meant to be. I just know that our paths will cross again."

"Me too, but can't you give me your address to be on the safe side, just in case they don't."

She laughed and said, "You really are so funny. I'll look forward to seeing you again very soon."

Suzy blew me a kiss and gave me a little wave, and I watched helplessly as she quickly made her way to the exit.

Should I have followed her? The last thing I wanted to do was to scare her.

By the time I arrived back at my bedsit I was in quite a confused state. As much as I tried to believe in what Suzy had said about fate and destiny, I was overcome with fear that I would never see her again. If she'd said she planned to go to The Manor House every night, then that would've been easy. She hadn't told me if she'd liked walking in Clissold Park, going for a drink in The Brownswood pub or eating in The Wimpy Bar. What if she'd gone to all of those places but not at the same time as me? What if I went to all of those places and never saw Suzy again? The agonizing despair of constantly missing each other by an hour or two, or perhaps minutes, was just too painful to even try and contemplate. All because fate had got its calculations just that little bit wrong.

Although it was difficult, I tried to be optimistic and convince myself that Suzy was bound to be there the next time Dantalian's Chariot played in London. So, the following Tuesday I went to a place called Klook's Kleek Railway Hotel, over in West Hampstead. I'd tried all the other places where I'd hoped to see Suzy over the previous few days, but she wasn't there either. Although I was now extremely distressed, I forced myself to carry on believing in fate and reminded myself that it had only been four days since I had last seen her. Of course, we would meet each other again, I just needed to trust in fate as much as Suzy did, which would then enable it to work.

From then on, I think I saw Dantalian's Chariot every time they played in London, right up to their last performance at Middle Earth, a small club in Covent Garden, in April 1968. They were excellent every time I saw them, but I never did quite enjoy it as much as I had on that night at The Manor House, that previous September. I continued to go and watch a lot of live music and was lucky enough to see a lot of wonderful American Psychedelic groups when they came over to London. Groups like The Byrds, The Electric Prunes, The Doors & The Jefferson Airplane. They generally played at The Roundhouse, and even though that venue was much larger than the usual clubs I went to, and also a lot darker, I always looked out for Suzy, hoping that she would in some way return to me in real life.

I eventually stopped going to see live music. It had all gone a bit too prog for my liking, and then it was all glam rock with screaming girls wetting their knickers over long haired men wearing make-up. I was pretty sure that sort of thing wouldn't have been Suzy's cup of tea. Around this time, I moved out of my bedsit and was able to buy a small house very close by. I'm still living there now, in fact. I've never really thought about leaving the area I've come to love and call home, even when it was quite dangerous here back in the eighties. What's more, I haven't ever given up believing in fate. As Suzy said, if it's meant to be it's meant to be. I'm sure I'll see her again, whether it's in this life or the next one. When I do, I will tell her what I found out in the library that Monday lunchtime, that 'Dantalian is the seventy first spirit, he is a duke, great and mighty, appearing in the form of a man with many countenances.'

Pawn Hub

Emily arrived home from work on that cold Friday evening feeling flustered and looking even more dishevelled than usual. "Hello Bernard, have you been worried about me?" Without waiting for an answer, she continued, "Have you been playing with your little tinkle balls again, all by yourself? Ah, aren't you clever?" Emily stood there expectantly, but there was still no response from Bernard. "Are you very cross with me, Bernard?" Emily asked. Bernard bemusedly looked up at this woman with sticking up hair and streaks of grime all over her face and thought 'What a ridiculous question. Of course, I am. I haven't had my dinner yet.'

"You must be very hungry. Mummy will get Bernard his nice dinner now, sorry to keep you waiting but Mummy has been stuck on the nasty, smelly tube for over an hour after somebody decided to jump in front of a train and ruin everybody else's weekend, as well as their own." There was still no sign of sympathy from Bernard, who was now even more confused because, although he hadn't seen her for some considerable time, he was fairly certain that his real Mummy had not resembled this woman in anyway whatsoever.

Emily loved Bernard very much and tolerated his behaviour a lot more than she would have done if he had been a man. If a man had scratched her new leather sofa for no good reason and then thrown up and pissed all over it, he would probably have found himself in considerably more trouble than Bernard had ever been in.

In fact, Emily, by and large, preferred cats to people. She knew exactly where she was with a cat. A cat wouldn't promise to phone her and then not bother. A cat had never sent her a succession of drunken, abusive text messages in the middle of the night saying how much they hated her. A cat wouldn't dream of inviting her to spend Christmas Day with their family and then send an e-mail on Boxing Day to say they'd forgotten. Not once had a cat ever said anything to Emily that was so horrible and hurtful that it had made her cry for days on end.

Emily opened a sachet of smelly, brown sludge which the label described as being, a 'specially prepared gourmet chicken dish that all cats were certain to adore' and served it in a dish marked 'Bernard's Din-Dins.' While Emily wasn't sure about the gourmet part or whether it actually contained any real chicken, her cat certainly seemed to adore it. She retrieved an almost spotless dish marked 'Bernard's Brekkie' from the floor, placed it in the dishwasher and announced, "Right, that's you all sorted Bernard, now its Mummy's turn to have a quick bite to eat before she goes out on her exciting date."

This was surprising news, and even Bernard stopped eating momentarily to look up from his dinner to make sure he'd heard correctly. Emily hadn't been on a date, exciting or otherwise, for many months now. Not since a man she'd last lived with decided to leave her. Emily had been extremely upset by this, mainly because the man hadn't really explained to her why he'd made the decision to go and find somebody much better than her. She was sure she hadn't done anything wrong, but she had agonized over and over in her head about the things that perhaps she might not have done quite right. All he had said to her was that it was a bad time for him at the moment, which had confused her no end. Did that mean that when it was a good time for him, he'd be back again? She doubted it very much, but it didn't stop her from hoping. Without hope, what else have you really got?

Anyway, that was all water under the bridge now, and Emily felt she was ready once again to dip her toe back in to the murky, polluted waters of romance. So, she'd joined up to one of those dating sites. All you had to do was upload a photograph of yourself and say what age group of man you were looking to meet and give a few other specific requirements that you would expect them to like, or be able to do, such as eat, listen, read, walk, laugh, enjoy the company of a cat and not mind too much if, on occasion, should they be the first to come home, there might be a peculiar smell coming from the sofa.

After finishing her light supper, Emily went for the obligatory pre date, 'shit, shower and shave.' She put on something nice to wear, which she had already chosen the previous night as soon as she'd received notification that Barry from Hackney Marshes was very interested and wanted to meet up for a drink. Emily was reluctant at first. Although she also lived in the borough of Hackney, Hackney Marshes was absolutely miles away and she would have to catch a whole fleet of differently numbered buses in order to get there. Even if she drove, it would take her over half an hour.

Don't worry about that yet, she thought, let's just see how the date goes first. Barry had suggested the Hackney Road as a good meeting point and said there were, as he put it, 'a lot of nice boozers down there.' Normally, she would be able to get within the vicinity of that destination relatively easily by tube. At Manor House, though, her nearest station, Emily assumed that they would still be scraping up what was left of the wretched person who had jumped in front of the train earlier. An inconsiderate act which had forced her and the rest of the passengers on her train to walk along the tracks in the tunnel in order to get out of the station. This also appeared to be the reason why there were no cabs available that evening. "I don't know, Bernard," she said, "some people just don't think of all the problems they will cause by throwing themselves in front of a train. If they have to do it, why not do it on Sunday morning or early Sunday afternoon at the latest, thus minimising the disruption to others and giving the cleaners ample time to tidy up the mess before the Monday morning rush hour begins."

Bernard, who was now sprawled out in his chair, looked up briefly, slowly shook his head from side to side and decided it wasn't worth getting involved.

Not wanting to cancel and therefore, miss a good opportunity to get back in the dating game, Emily decided she would drive from her flat in Woodberry Down over to one of these nice boozers on the Hackney Road. Unfortunately, this would mean that she wouldn't be able to have a proper drink. Emily wasn't a big drinker by any stretch of fancy, but she wouldn't have minded something to help calm her nerves.

* * *

Emily arrived at the meeting point, which was a pub called The Mary Wollstonecraft, and luckily managed to find a parking space not too far away. She took a few deep breaths then checked her face in the rear-view mirror. Hopefully, she thought, she looks the same in real life now as she did in that photograph she had submitted to the dating site. It was only a few years old, and she didn't think she had changed too drastically. Barry obviously liked the way she looked, and even if nothing came of this, it felt so good to know that somebody else found you attractive again. She took another look at the photograph of Barry she had printed out. There were actually three men in the picture, all sitting in a pub. He had specified that he was the one on the left and the other two in the picture were his mates. He had also added, very chivalrously, not to worry about arranging a set time to meet, as he was going to go to the pub straight from work and would already be there whenever she arrived.

The first thing that struck Emily as she walked into the pub, was a pool ball that somebody had miscued while attempting a difficult shot on the pool table positioned close to the front door.

"Oh, sorry Love, are you alright?" said the man, whose manic shot had caused the pool ball to strike Emily fiercely on one of her breasts, and who she now recognized as her date, Barry.

"Urgh, yes. Don't worry it's alright," she replied, trying to hide her discomfort and the fact that she was in some considerable pain. "Is your name Barry by any chance?" she asked.

"Shit! You must be Emily? I'm really sorry about that. I'll get you a drink in a minute. Let me just finish this game. It shouldn't be too long."

Emily stood patiently beside the pool table watching Barry play pool for the next ten minutes. We will laugh about this one day, she thought, as the last ball was finally potted.

"Right, what are you having then?" Barry said, making his way to the bar.

"Can I just have an orange juice and lemonade, please?"

"Don't you drink?"

"I'm driving."

"Great."

They took their drinks and found a suitably vacant table to sit down at.

"So, here we are," Emily said, looking directly into Barry's eyes.

"Yes. How's your, er, you know?" asked Barry, looking directly at Emily's chest area.

"Yes, it's fine, thanks."

"Good. I'm glad I didn't do it any damage, it's very nice. In fact, they both are, if you don't mind me saying so."

"Not at all."

"I suppose if I hadn't just met you, I could offer to kiss it better."

"That's a very kind thing to say."

"I'm serious. They look a lot better in real life than they did in that picture you sent me."

"Thank you. So, you came here straight from work, then? What is it you do?" Emily enquired, hoping to change the subject as she was starting to feel a little uncomfortable.

"Let's not talk about work, it's boring. It's Friday, we're free to do what we want to do. Let's enjoy ourselves. Another orange juice and lemonade?"

"No, it's ok, I've still got this one, thanks."

While Barry went to the bar the get himself another drink, Emily began to take stock of the situation. I know I haven't been on a date for a fair while, she thought, but are people now usually this forward when they first meet you? I suppose in one way he did have a bit of a lever to start mentioning my breasts and didn't just start talking about them willy-nilly. Then again, maybe he manipulated the whole conversation by hitting that pool ball at me on purpose. It's not unfeasible that he could have recognised me through the window as I was about to enter the pub, and as soon as I was inside, aimed that shot right at me. He might have been practicing it all evening before I got here, for all I know. That would explain why he wanted to get here early. On the other hand, he does seem quite nice, and it makes a pleasant change to have somebody complimenting me once again. I definitely need to keep an eye on the proceedings, though. He might be one of those men you hear about who are really only after one thing, and certainly not looking to settle down in a happy, loving relationship at all.

Barry returned from the bar and placed his pint of beer and what looked like a double Scotch on the table. "I decided that if you didn't want one, I'll have yours," he said, laughing as he meticulously positioned himself besides Emily.

Once Barry was comfortable, Emily asked, "Have you been on this dating site very long?"

"No, I only joined it last night, what about you?" he replied.

"A week, or so," Emily lied. "So, what made you join it, then?"

"I don't know. What about you?"

"Oh, you know, I thought it was time to try something different. Perhaps, these days, this is the easiest way to meet somebody."

"You can say that again. It was definitely easy."

"Aw, that's a really nice thing to say."

"Look, why don't we finish these drinks and go to this party I've been invited to," said Barry, changing the subject. "All of my mates are going to be there."

"Where is it?"

"Only about a quarter of an hour's drive away, near Mabley Green. We can stop off on the way and get some booze in."

"I won't be able to drink, though."

"Don't worry about that. Leave the car when we get to the party and enjoy yourself. It's Friday, we're free, to do what we want to do."

"Alright, I'll come to the party for a little while, but I won't drink. I need to take my cat to the vet early tomorrow morning, he's been displaying some very strange tendencies," said Emily, quite flattered that this man, with such a carefree spirit who, even though he'd not long met her, was already keen for her to spend the night with him and didn't mind her meeting all of his friends first, either. Maybe this whole dating site carry-on really was a lot easier than she'd ever imagined it would be. "Do you like cats, Barry?"

"They're alright," Barry replied, knocking back both of his drinks. "Come on, let's go, we need to get to Costcutters before it shuts."

* * *

Once they'd arrived at Mabley Green, Emily parked her car outside a block of flats and looked around. "I don't think I've ever been here before," she said. "Was that a stone circle we passed a little while ago?"

"Yeah, I think so but there's only one of them left now," Barry replied.

"Oh, no, that's such a shame. What happened to all the other stones?"

"I don't know. They probably got bombed during the Blitz. This whole area was a major target during the war."

Emily smiled, not at the thought of Mabley Green and the surrounding areas of Hackney being bombed by the Luftwaffe, but because she admired intelligent men who took an interest in their local history.

As they walked the short distance to the entrance of the flats, Emily went to hold Barry's hand. "Not yet," he said, "we're almost there." They got into a waiting lift and Barry pressed the button for the 12th Floor.

"That's fortunate," said Emily.

"What is?" said Barry.

"One floor higher and your friends would be on the 13th Floor."

"So what?"

"It's unlucky. We wouldn't want our first night out together to be cursed with bad luck."

"That sounds like a right load of old bollocks. I don't believe in superstition. I've broken loads of mirrors in my time, some of them on purpose, and it hasn't done me any harm."

As the lift door opened, the muffled sound of music could be heard coming from one of the flats. Barry had to ring the doorbell several times before a man who looked like he had just woken up, partially opened the door, and very slowly said, "Hello?"

"It's me, Barry. You met me last week when I was in that pub with Zoe."

"Oh, yeah, you were with Zoe in that pub last week."

"That's right. You invited us both. Is Zoe here yet?"

"No, not yet. Come in."

"Hello, I'm Emily."

"Hello Emily, you weren't in the pub last week, were you? Do you know Zoe as well, then? said the tired looking man.

"No. I'm looking forward to meeting her later along with all of Barry's other friends."

"How many other people has he invited then?"

"None," said Barry quickly, and made his way to the kitchen to drop off the carrier bag of alcohol he had recently bought. Turning to Emily, he said, "Help yourself to a drink and make yourself at home, I just need to go to the toilet for a little while."

Emily found a big bottle of some supermarket brand cola in the fridge and fixed herself a non-alcoholic drink. She then made her way to the living room where all the other guests appeared to be congregating. There were six other people present who were all sitting cross legged on the floor in a loose circle. "Hello, I'm Emily. What are you guys up to?"

"We're about to start chasing the dragon," one of them replied.

"That sounds like fun. Is it a game?" Emily enquired.

"It's much better than any game. It's smoking heroin. Would you like to try it?" said another person.

"Oh, no thanks, I'd better not, I'm driving," said Emily.

At that moment the doorbell rang, and Barry came running into the living room, still pulling up his jeans and adjusting his belt. "There's someone at the door," he said, as he rushed over to Emily, guided her over to the unoccupied sofa, sat her down and put his arm around her.

"Well, can't you answer it?" said the sleepy man.

"I can't. It's not my flat and I'm comfortable here now," Barry replied, leaning even closer to Emily while lifting her arm and putting it around him.

The sleepy man tutted and got up off the floor as the doorbell continued to ring. He slowly opened the door, "Hello Zoe, good to see you. Come in," he said.

When the sleepy man returned to the living room, he was followed by a woman and a man holding hands. "What the fuck are you doing here? I was right, I knew you'd be here and who the fuck is that slag?" Zoe said, looking in the direction of the sofa.

"And who the fuck is that shit-cunt?" Barry shouted.

"None of your fucking business," screamed Zoe.

"It is my fucking business, you're my fucking girlfriend," yelled Barry.

"No, I'm not. After last night, I can do what I like. We've split up now, remember," Zoe yelled back.

"Can somebody please tell me what's going on? Barry? I thought you and I were going to have a serious go at having a relationship," said Emily.

"Sorry Love, if you think you and me are going to have a relationship, you're barking up the wrong tree."

"So, this woman means nothing to you," said Zoe, in a much lower tone.

"Nothing at all. She's not fit to lace your boots. And what about this shit-cunt you're with?" said Barry.

"You're joking, aren't you? I wouldn't go out with him for all the tea in China. He means absolutely fuck all to me."

Emily had already got up from the sofa and was running towards the front door. The tears were streaming down her face, and she felt as if she might be sick at any moment. It wasn't until the lift arrived and she was about to get in that she became aware of another presence behind her. As soon as they were both in the lift, she recognized the man who had recently arrived with the woman called Zoe.

"Are you going to be, okay?" the man asked, once the lift started descending.

"Yes. Thanks. I just feel completely stupid," Emily sobbed.

"I know the feeling," he sighed.

"I think we both might have been used."

"You could be right. They were kissing each other just before I decided that it was probably time I should be going."

They travelled the last few floors in mutual silence. As they came out of the building into the cold, uncaring night, Emily realised that in her desperation to get away she had left her coat behind. I'm not going back for it, she decided, they've probably already put it on e-bay by now. After composing herself, she said, "My car is parked over there, can I give you a lift anywhere?"

"I only live in Dalston. That's really nice of you, but Hackney Wick station isn't too far away. I could probably do with clearing my head a bit as well. Plus, I wouldn't mind taking another look at what's left of that stone circle they've got here."

"To be honest, you would be doing me a favour. I'm not sure I want to drive back on my own all confused again trying to work out why some people have to be so horrible to others."

"I know exactly what you mean. Sometimes I think the more kindness I try to show people, the more they take me for granted. It's almost as if they want to punish me because I'm different or they think I must be weak."

They got into Emily's car, and once they had made their getaway from the place they were both glad to see the back of, the man continued, "People say I'm too sensitive and that's why I get hurt. They even say I'm too honest. Can you believe that? I mean what am I supposed to do, not care about people and constantly lie to them? Why should I have to be the same as nearly everybody else?"

"Just because you are in the minority, it doesn't mean you're wrong," replied Emily. "Maybe if more people were like you, the world wouldn't be such a terrible place. You must never stop being honest. Eventually, you will meet somebody who is also the same as you and who will love you for who you are. Do you like cats, by the way?"

"I absolutely adore cats, even though sometimes they can do some very unusual things," he replied, with a little chuckle. Placing his hand on his forehead, he continued, "What was it that Albert Schweitzer said? 'There are two means of refuge from the miseries of life: music and cats.'"

"Yes, I think I read that in his review of the musical in The Hackney Gazette. Isn't it amazing? I've seen it nine times already and loved absolutely every single minute. It's so true to life. Perhaps we could go and see it together sometime," said Emily, looking towards the man and smiling affectionately.

The man smiled back and said, "Has anybody ever told you, you've got fantastic bosoms?"

Kiss Goodbye To All That

I wasn't as desperate to get home as the others, and I hung around for as long I could, but I suppose I had to bite the bullet sometime. To be honest, the thought of seeing her again terrified me, even though I'd seen some pretty horrific things over the past four years. It's still difficult to imagine how I managed to survive the whole sorry affair, but I did, which is more than can be said for a lot of other poor souls. Was it luck? Who knows? I can't say I've ever really considered myself lucky before.

I never gave much consideration to volunteering either. All the other clerks where I worked were doing it, and I didn't want to be the only one left behind. So, we all marched down to the recruiting office that afternoon in September 1914, like a load of silly children, formed a long queue and anxiously waited to see if we'd be accepted. I imagine everybody felt the same and was dreading the embarrassment of being turned away because they weren't up to scratch. I was hugely relieved when I passed my medical, given a shilling and told I was fit for service. I assumed I had nothing to lose by giving it a shot. I wouldn't be missing out on anything back home, and even if I ended up regretting it, everybody said it would all be over by Christmas anyway.

Once the tedious months of training were finally over, I could hardly wait to be sent overseas. It had become clear that perhaps winning this war wasn't going to be as easy as everybody had first thought, although by now, I just wanted a change of scenery and a chance to be able to put into practice everything I'd been taught.

I'd never been to France before and at first was quite surprised to find that it wasn't that different from the English countryside I had visited once or twice on a family outing as a child. Then I got the shock of my life when I arrived at the front. I can't imagine anybody having ever been anywhere like that before. Not even in their worst nightmares.

I was told in June 1916 that my turn had come around for leave and I would have ten days to go and spend back in England. Although I had nothing to go back to, I couldn't wait to get away from that place. The first thing I did when I got home was take off my uniform and soak myself in a hot bath. It was the most pleasure I'd experienced since I'd joined up to become a soldier. There was no point in regretting volunteering; I would have been conscripted by now, in any case, and I'd probably be over there being shelled and shot at right at that very moment, instead of lying in that glorious bath.

I dressed into my best clothes and admired myself in the mirror. All in all, I didn't think I looked too terrible. Stepping out onto the peaceful streets of Kingsland Road felt good, and it was a relief not to have to worry about somebody trying to kill you. I had developed a taste for alcohol over in France and decided to treat myself to a pint of English beer, if only to compare it to all the French beer I'd been drinking. I walked in to my local, The Butcher's Arms, and that's when I first set eyes on Ivy. She looked directly at me and gave me the nicest smile anybody has ever given me. I was fairly certain they were her real teeth as well. I had never been in love before and wouldn't know what to expect, but at that moment, the world seemed to come to a halt and nothing else mattered except that I had to be with this girl. Unfortunately, I had no idea how I was going to go about doing this, but Ivy made it easy for me.

"Hello, I haven't seen you in here before, have I?" she said.

"No, most likely not. I've never set foot in a pub in England before," I replied. "Can I offer to buy you a drink?"

"I would very much like that, but you'd better not. You know it's against the law to buy alcohol for other people in a pub now?"

"Is it? I had no idea. There are a few people I've seen who would be very happy to hear that, I can tell you."

"Thanks all the same but I shall buy myself one before they close."

"Did you say close? It's only a quarter past nine by my watch."

"The pubs all close at half past nine now. Where have you been hiding?"

"France."

"Oh, are you French? You speak very good English."

"No, not at all. I'm from round here in De Beauvoir. I've been over in France fighting in the war."

"I see. I'm sorry, have you been injured? You're not wearing your uniform."

"No, I couldn't wait to get the bloody thing off, if you'll pardon my French."

Fortunately, Ivy wasn't offended and gave me another smile. We ordered our drinks separately and I drank my first pint of English beer. It was disgusting. Like drinking a pint of warm water, and not cheap in anyone's book. "Are you here by yourself, then?" I asked her, placing the beer back down on the bar with a disdainful look on my face.

"At this moment in time, yes, and I can see you don't approve."

"No, I think it's wonderful that you are all on your own."

She laughed, introduced herself and shook my hand. As my hand touched Her's, I felt an explosive surge of energy take over my whole body and I then became aware of a hollow sensation in the pit of my stomach. I hadn't experienced anything like that before in my entire life.

I was soon brought back down to earth by the sound of a bell ringing loudly which caused me turn around in a state of shock. Behind the bar the landlord shouted, "Time ladies & gentlemen, please, you horrible people. Don't you know there's a war on? Yes, it breaks my heart as well, but rules are rules."

"Stick the rules up your arse and fuck right off," somebody shouted from somewhere, and everybody laughed before they slowly began to make their way out of the pub.

I asked Ivy if I could accompany her back to where she lived, which happened to be on my way home, and she very kindly agreed to meet me again in a couple of days to go for a walk. That Saturday couldn't come around quick enough. All I could do was to think of Ivy every minute of the day and night. Even though I had never seen a real woman in the nude before, I tried to imagine Ivy standing naked before me. Her beautiful body and the softness of her skin as I held her in my arms.

At long last, Saturday arrived. I had another bath and put on my best suit again, hoping Ivy wouldn't notice it was the same one I was wearing when I last saw her. It was a glorious June day when I left the house and walked the short distance to where Ivy lived. I knocked on her front door and stood waiting, feeling quite apprehensive. As soon as she opened the door, she gave me that marvellous smile, and I felt completely relaxed. We walked, talked and laughed and I had never felt more comfortable being with somebody. For the first time in my life, I didn't want to be anywhere else in the world. This was the happiest I had ever been, and it seemed like maybe life was worth living after all.

Nothing could spoil that day, even when we decided to get the tram up to Finsbury Park and go to the Empire. We saw Fanny

Farthing from Clitheroe, who was a wonderful singer. She got the entire audience to join in and sing along to a couple of the very popular songs of the time: 'We Don't Want To Lose You, But We Think You Ought To Go', and 'Let's Have A Fight With Them Cowardly Conchies, Because We All Want To Knock One Out.' There was also, Whit Cuncliffe, who was very comical and had the catchphrase 'Did you come on the tram?' Then there was the incredible, Wee Jock McTavish who was Scotch, and pretended to be a kid as he was only four feet nine, had a high-pitched voice and some very childlike features; and finally, the awfully talented Alfred Mattock, who played the trombone blindfolded whilst riding a bicycle up and down the stage.

Anyway, Ivy and I were on the tram talking and laughing when we were rudely interrupted by a woman who approached me. "Can I give this gift to a brave soldier?" she said, presenting me with a white feather in front of everybody else. I was speechless and embarrassed, as I don't like being the centre of attention at the best of times, but Ivy was incredibly supportive.

"What do you think you're doing?" she shouted at the woman, "And what the hell is this?" she continued, grabbing the feather from me and holding it aloft. "Is this from that dodo that lives up your crump hole? You should be ashamed of yourself. This brave man has been fighting over in France. Why don't *you* go over there? As soon as the Germans see your ugly face they're bound to surrender." Everybody on the tram was laughing and ridiculing this woman and she quickly tried to get off. I had never felt so proud to be with somebody as I was at that particular moment.

I continued to see Ivy every day after that for the rest of my leave. It was painful saying good night to her in the evening, and I could hardly wait to see her the next day. I was so happy I'd met somebody I loved being with. We'd constantly laugh together and sometimes we didn't even need to say anything. It was almost as if we could read each other's minds.

The dreaded last day of my leave arrived, and the thought of not seeing Ivy for who knows how long, if at all, was terrifying. I tried to put on a brave face and didn't want to appear too maudlin on our last day together. Hopefully we could carry on enjoying what was left of our precious time.

Once the pub had closed that night, I walked Ivy back to where she lived. Although Ivy was gaily talking away, I was finding it difficult to be chatty. As we turned into Downham Road, Ivy looked at me and said, "You're very quiet tonight, Harold. Are you feeling alright?"

"Yes, I'm fine. I was just thinking that I'll really miss you."

"And I shall miss you too. I've had such a lovely time with you."

"I'm not sure I can leave you and go back to that place."

"You must. You can't do a bunk, can you? They'll shoot you. We'll see each other again when you get back. Everybody says It'll all be over by Christmas."

"I hope so. Will you write to me, please?"

"Of course I will."

I went to kiss her, but she pushed me away. I stood there confused and uncomfortable, wondering if I had ruined everything. "I'm so sorry, Ivy. I just wanted to kiss you as I don't know when I'll see you again. If at all."

Ivy stood looking at me. After a short while she broke the silence. "Look, Harold, I really like you and you are such a wonderful friend, but I think you might have the wrong idea about us."

"Oh, I thought you were going to be my sweetheart," I said, and could feel the tears start to well up in my eyes. I wish they hadn't, but everything had happened so quickly, and it was all too much of a shock.

"I'm so sorry, I've really upset you, haven't I?" said Ivy.

"No, of course not," I lied. I desperately needed to get away and be on my own, but something stopped me from moving. Perhaps I hoped that Ivy would change her mind there and then and make everything alright again. At that moment the whole world seemed to be spinning around, out of control, and it felt as if my soul had been ripped out my body. The last thing I needed was somebody to walk past and start interfering.

"That's right, Miss. You tell him. A coward like that doesn't deserve to have a pretty girl like you. You should be with a real man who wants to fight for his country, not some shirker," said a short man in his early forties.

This time, I didn't wait for Ivy to stand up for me. I also didn't bother to think up some witty admonition, either. Instead, I swung around and gave the little nosy-parker a terrific punch with all of what was left of my strength. He fell backwards and smashed his head on the road.

When I noticed he didn't appear to be moving, I ran off back to where I lived. I stayed awake all night worrying about losing Ivy, the possibility that I'd killed a man, and having to return to the trenches in France first thing in the morning. As I'm sure you'll appreciate, getting a good night's sleep was never going to be a straightforward affair.

* * *

Once I became aware of the greyness of dawn enclosing the room, I knew it was time for me to make my way overseas and be a soldier again, expected to kill people I didn't know who didn't know me. Back to the eternal marching and the continuous digging and living in the ground with the lice, the flies and the rats with the stench of vomit, piss, shit and death all around. Trying to steer clear of the bullets, the gas, the bombs and the shells. Hearing the incessant explosions and seeing the blood, the mutilated bodies, and the rotting corpses. The devastation and destruction everywhere. Back to the screaming, the crying and the fear. In simple terms, I was returning to war.

At least I wouldn't have to stay and see Ivy walking arm in arm and laughing with another man. Somebody she'd rather be with, who she obviously thinks is better than me. Also, there was the possibility that I might be hanged for murder, so perhaps I was better off scarpering over to France after all. I put on my uniform again for the first time in ten days and set off, feeling the lowest I had ever felt in my entire life. I couldn't get what happened on that last night with Ivy out of my mind. I spent every second of the journey going over the time we had spent together, remembering every conversation we'd had, the laughter we'd shared and all the smiles she'd given me.

Several days after I was back in France, the post arrived, and I wondered if I would receive a letter from Ivy. Perhaps she had thought things over and had now reconsidered her decision. Just one sentence from her saying that would make me the happiest man in all the world, but, as usual, there was nothing for me. Maybe it had got lost, though everybody else in my battalion seemed to have received a letter or parcel from home.

There wasn't a single day during the rest of the time I was in that place when I wasn't constantly thinking of Ivy. It certainly got me through some of the hellish times. I'd sometimes think that

Kiss Goodbye To All That

maybe if I got wounded quite badly, maybe lost an arm or a leg, or perhaps both arms or both legs, or even both arms and both legs, like some poor basket cases I saw, Ivy might feel sorry for me and decide to be my sweetheart. I assumed she'd probably draw the line at me having part of my head, face or Gentlemen's area blown off. I was certain that deep down she still liked me, as she hadn't given my name to the police for killing that irritating man. If she had, they would have come for me by now and taken me to prison to hang me. Perhaps that's why she couldn't write to me, in case they traced the letter, which would lead to my immediate arrest. I knew Ivy was clever and wouldn't want to get me into any trouble. On other days, when I was feeling down, I believed Ivy had told the police everything and they were just waiting for the war to be over first before arresting me. It was all a bit worrying, and I kept myself to myself and fortunately, everybody else was happy to leave me alone with my thoughts.

I remember overhearing, on that cold, dark, morning of 11th November 1918, that an armistice had been signed at 5am. The war would be over at 11am that day. Most soldiers seemed relieved that they wouldn't have to be forced to go over the top anymore and kill men who were just like us but happened to be from another country. There would no longer be that constant feeling of either awaiting death or avoiding death. Everybody thought that all they had to do was sit tight in the rain with mud up to their arses for another six hours, and the horror would finally be over.

Six hours can seem like a long time when orders have been received to carry on fighting. We continued to fire a load of shells over at the other lot and received a fair few back at us in return. It seemed like everybody was firing every shell they could get their hands on. Perhaps they were trying to use them all up to save having to carry them all the way back home, especially as there would be no use for them considering that this was the war to end all wars.

Once everything had quietened down around our section of the trench, everybody, who still had one, started looking at their watches. We were peacefully sitting around smoking when our Sergeant-Major, this mad Geordie, decided there was suitable time for one more trench raid. "Come on you right lazy bunch of fuckers, it's your last chance to get some Huns. Private Ward, you'll volunteer as always, won't you laddie?"

I agreed, thinking what have I got to lose? I'm sure to be arrested in a few hours' time, so what difference does it make if I get killed now or hanged when I get home? The Seargeant-Major rounded up four others who were a lot more reluctant to volunteer and had to be threatened, and off we crept, under cover of darkness, into no man's land towards what was left of an enemy trench. When we reached our destination, we waited, listening out for any strange voices. The unusual silence suggested that the trench had most likely been abandoned, and we climbed in.

The stench was overwhelming. It was the all-too-familiar, sweet, sickly odour of decomposing corpses. We realised from the squelching noises we heard as our feet hit the ground that we were standing on what was left of these neglected bodies.

"Fucking hell, this is fucking disgusting. Can't we just go home?" someone said, examining the sole of his boot.

"No, we fucking can't." The Sergeant-Major replied. "The war's not over yet and it's not too late to have you court-martialed and shot for disobeying orders. We are going to check this place out thoroughly to make sure there isn't anybody hiding here."

"There's nobody here. They've all gone to better place. Like Hell, perhaps," someone else said.

"Did you not hear me? Maybe we should cut out the court-martial, and I'll just execute you right here, instead. Your orders are to search this trench. Now get moving."

After we'd made our way through the mud and the discarded debris of the disused trench, somebody else tried to reason with the Sergeant-Major, "It's all quiet. There's nothing alive here except rats and it's starting to get light now as well."

In the murky dawn light, the Sergeant-Major was now visibly distressed at the thought of there being no more enemy soldiers to fight. He paced up and down, reluctant to abort his unsuccessful mission. In a last act of desperation, he shouted out "OI, CUNTS! WHERE ARE YOU? COME OUT HERE NOW AND SHOW YOURSELF"

A bedraggled looking man, who was about the same age as me, appeared from under a pile of dead bodies where he'd been hiding, and announced, "Ja, Ich bin Soldat Kuntz. Komrade. Komrade." He had both of his arms raised, and in one hand was a creased photograph he had been clutching. He lowered his arms and held the photograph towards us with both hands so that we could see the picture. It was of a young woman holding a baby. He smiled at us, "Es ist zu Ende. Komrade"

The Sergeant-Major ordered us to aim our rifles and the man tried to run away, "Nein bitte, Komrade," he shouted. Six shots were fired in his direction and the man crumpled to the ground. I watched the photograph slowly disappear beneath the mud as I stood there thinking of Ivy.

"He would have done the same to us given half a chance," said the Sergeant-Major, before adding, "Let's not do anything stupid. Make sure we make our way back carefully and keep an eye out for any more Huns."

We walked in silence through the heavy mist, which lay like smoke above the concealed ground, and arrived back in our trench. At exactly 11am there was an eerie silence, and nobody was quite sure what to do next. I just sat there awaiting my fate.

Eventually, the time came when I had to return home. I wasn't arrested and, so far, I haven't seen Ivy with anybody else either. Maybe I am lucky after all. Although this flu that's going around, that everyone thinks has come from Spain, has made me feel like I'm at death's door. But If I can survive the past four years, I'm sure I can survive anything. I'm really looking forward to starting a completely new life. Maybe there's even a chance Ivy and I will be together again, and, who knows, this time it could be forever.

Possessions

The Joseph Conrad pub in Stoke Newington was a little quieter than usual for a Sunday night. One of the regulars had unexpectedly died that week. Over in the corner of the pub was a table full of various pieces of framed memorabilia. These included an Arsenal shirt, a Tottenham Hotspur shirt, and a Leyton Orient shirt (which may or may not have been genuinely signed by the players), along with various signed photos of local celebrities who were all household names. People such as TV Presenter Gaz Top, Radio DJ Nick Grimshaw, Pop band Cornershop's Tijinder Singh and Comedian Stewart Lee. At the very front of the table was a picture of the deceased, placed there by his friends, not only to show who the auction was for but also as a fitting tribute to their sadly departed companion.

"What's all that about?" Rob asked the landlord, nodding towards the prize-laden table while waiting for his drink.

"Oh, that's an auction for Reg. It's to help pay for his funeral. If there's anything you want, you place a bid in a sealed envelope and the highest bid wins it," replied the landlord.

"What did he die of?"

"He fell out of a window."

"Okay. I'll go and have a look, see if there's anything that takes my fancy," said Rob, taking a sip of his pint and collecting his change.

Rob made his way over to the table bearing the auction desirables, which was next to a group of mournful looking people sitting expectantly, in silence. He began to examine the items on offer one by one.

"I ain't got a clue who some of these people are," Rob said out loud to nobody. While looking around and holding aloft one of the framed photographs, he enquired, "Who's this cunt?"

"That's Reg," replied the landlord.

"Oh right, I didn't think I recognised him, and he ain't signed it either," he said, placing the picture carefully back down on the table and noticing he was getting some sinister looks from the people sitting nearby. Deciding there was nothing on show that he was desperate to own, he went to find a table on the other side of the pub.

"You don't mind if I sit here, do you?" Rob said to a man in his forties who was nursing a small amount of lager in his glass.

The man shook his head.

"I'm Rob, how you doing?"

"Alright."

"You don't look it, if you don't mind me saying so. You look like you're at the end of your tether, or at the end of something, anyway," Rob said, once he was seated. "Have you been to look at all that shit for sale over on that table?" he continued.

"No, I'm broke."

"How come? You spunked all your wages up the wall like everybody else?"

"No, I'm not working at the moment," replied the man.

"I thought as much, that's why I might be able to help you out. Let me get you another pint. I take it you're on the cheap rubbish."

When Rob returned, he said to the man, "How would you like to make some easy money?"

"It all depends on what I've got to do."

"It doesn't look like you've got much choice in the matter. You look pretty desperate to me, and I can guarantee you that later tonight, you'll be well on the way to being absolutely minted. More money than I'd wager you've seen in a very long while."

"Is it legal?"

"Of course, it's not. How do you think you can make a load of money legally in just a couple of hours?"

"If I knew that I wouldn't be sitting in here, would I?"

"Are you interested, or not?"

"What have I got to do?"

"Alright, I reckon I can trust you. There's a house I've been keeping an eye on for a couple of days. Nice secluded spot round the back of the cemetery. There're never any lights on, and not a living soul has gone in or come out of there since I've been watching it, so I reckon that whoever lives there must be on holiday."

"What? You want me to break in to a house?"

"No, I'll do the breaking in, you can be my assistant."

"Who do you think I am, Debbie McGee? What do you need an assistant for?"

"To carry things. It's a lot easier if there's two of us."

"Have you done this before?"

"Loads of times. It's a piece of piss."

"What if we get caught?"

"Just do everything I tell you to do, and we won't."

Rob looked at his watch and took another sip of his pint. He looked around the pub and leant over towards the man, before asking "Do you know any of those miserable fuckers sitting by that table full of junk?"

"Why?"

"There's something a bit weird about them. They aren't very friendly, either. They gave me some right evil looks when I was over there. At least you're sociable. So, what do I call you."

"You can call me Nick, if you want."

"OK, Nick. So, tell me. How come you look so miserable?"

"You know. The usual. It's personal. Just tell me where and when we're going to do this robbery."

"Alright, not so fast and keep your voice down. Meet me outside Stoke Newington train station at exactly midnight tonight."

"Midnight?"

"Yeah, it's not like you've got to worry about getting up early for work in the morning, is it? Everything'll be pretty much dead by then, and it gives me enough time to go and get all of my apparatus." Rob drained his pint and stood up. "Make sure you're there and don't be late, or you'll be the loser," he said as a parting shot before walking out the pub door.

* * *

When Nick arrived at midnight, Rob was nowhere to be seen. Nick walked all around the outside of the closed station before Rob finally appeared from the adjacent alleyway. "I just wanted to make sure you hadn't been followed," said Rob. "I'm a professional, see. I always consider every probable possibility. Right, let's go and get rich. Follow me. Today, my friend, is your lucky day."

They crossed the road and around ten minutes later had made their way to the house which had been the recent focus of Rob's surveillance. Rob led the way to the back window and stopped to put down his black holdall. He unzipped the bag and took out a couple of pairs of black gloves, a large screwdriver and a hammer. "Here, put these on," he said to Nick, passing him a pair of gloves. "Professional, see. I bet you didn't think of that, did you? Nobody will have a clue who we are."

Rob began trying to prise open the window with his chosen tools. After twenty minutes had passed, Nick said, "I thought you said you'd done this before."

"I have. I told you, I'm a professional," replied Rob, as he repeatedly hit the screwdriver against the bottom of the window with his hammer.

"Shush! You'll wake everybody up," whispered Nick, who was now beginning to curse his luck and wonder what he'd ever done to deserve to be so desperate that he had to resort to this.

"This window won't budge. Some stupid twat has painted it shut. I reckon we'll have to break the back door window and get in that way," said Rob, looking in his bag for something more suitable for the task in hand.

"But someone might hear and call the police."

Of course, they won't. It's London, isn't it? Nobody's going to get involved, especially at this time on a Sunday night when they're all in bed. I'll be quick," Rob said, before smashing the back door window pane with a slightly bigger hammer than the one he was using before. He put in his arm to unlock the door from the inside and turning to Nick with a big grin on his face, said, "Leave it to the experts."

Once they were in the house, Rob put on a head torch he had retrieved from his bag. "Right, let's look around for valuable stuff that's easy to carry. "The best bet is the bedroom; we might get a bit of tomfoolery in there if we're lucky," he said, making his way up the stairs as if it were his own house. Nick followed sheepishly behind hoping that this whole sorry episode would soon be over.

Rob opened a door at the far end of the landing and walked in. "Fucking hell, there's somebody in here," he said, turning around and running straight into Nick, knocking him to the floor.

"I thought you said everybody was on holiday," Nick whispered, once they had both reached the bottom of the stairs.

"Be quiet. Can you hear anything?" Rob said a little while later, having recomposed himself.

"No, but let's get out of here before we get arrested."

"Hold your horses. There was somebody in bed, some old woman, but she can't have woken up."

"How old?"

"I don't know, about fifty-six or fifty-seven. Maybe she's deaf."

"I don't care what she is, I can't do this if somebody's here. I'm leaving before the police arrive."

"Look, we can't go yet. We've put a lot of effort into this and have come too far to turn back now. It's just a woman asleep on her own. All we have to do is tie her up. I've got a bit of old rope in my bag. There's a blindfold in there as well. She'll be none the wiser who we are when she wakes up in the morning. Come on, let's go back upstairs, get what we want, and leave"

"What if she wakes up and starts screaming?"

"I've got a special contraption to put in her mouth that will keep her quiet. I've used it loads of times before and it never fails. Come on, what are you waiting for, doomsday? We haven't got all night."

They ascended the stairs for a second time, but noticeably with more caution than before. They tiptoed into the bedroom and made their way towards the bed. Rob decided to apply the blindfold to the woman first, using the logic that if she did happen to wake up, at least she wouldn't be able to give a visual description of them both to the police. When he had finished, he turned round to Nick and whispered, "You see, she's completely dead to the world. Let's tie her up though, just in case. You take a look in those drawers in that bedside cabinet over there while I'm doing this. Save us a bit of time later."

Without the benefit of a headtorch, Nick found it difficult to see in the oppressive darkness of the room, and clumsily knocked over a bedside lamp which went crashing to the floor. Rob instinctively stopped tying the woman up and took a few steps backwards, expecting the inevitable. Once he had realized that the woman had still not moved, he hissed, "For crying out loud. What are you trying to do, wake the dead? It's a good job she's a heavy sleeper."

"Are you sure she is just asleep?" Nick whispered.

"I've got no idea. Tell you what, I'll give her a bit of a shake."

"But that might wake her up."

"Alright, I tell you what we'll do. I'll finish tying her up and then I'll put that gadget in her mouth. She's already blindfolded so if she does wake up when I give her a little jiggle, she won't be able to do anything anyway."

When Rob had finished fully securing the woman, he placed both hands on her shoulders and gently shook her from side to side. In a soothing voice he said, "Hello dear, are you awake? Time to wake up, love." After his attempt to rouse the woman had been unsuccessful, he turned round and said, "Fucking hell, she's proper dead."

"Right, that's it, I'm going. We need to report this. We have to notify the authorities. There's a dead woman in bed on her own," Nick said.

"Wait. Everybody just needs to calm down. Let's have a look around, see what she's left, fill our boots and get the fuck out of here."

"What about reporting the dead body to the police."

"The police? Oh sure, we'll just walk into the nearest cop shop and say 'Excuse me officer we've just been to burgle this woman's house and it would appear that she's now dead.' They'll do us for murder and robbery, lock us up and throw away the key. That's if we're lucky and they're in a good mood."

"But we haven't done anything."

"It doesn't matter. You can't trust them. Why do you think everybody calls them the filth? As soon as we walk into Stoke Newington Police station, they'll shoot us both dead with a shotgun and say it was us that committed suicide. And do you want to know something that's even more frightening? They'd get away with it, as well."

"Surely, they could tell it wasn't us that killed her by estimating how long she's been dead?"

"It can't be that long; she doesn't smell that bad. Then again, it is bloody cold in here, even with gloves on."

"We need to put everything back in its place, exactly how it was, leave quietly, and phone the hospital anonymously to report a dead body. It's the decent thing to do."

"What about the broken window? Who's going to fix that?"

"I thought you might have something in your holdall."

"I can't carry everything around, can I? I'll tell you what we'll do. Let's sweep up the broken glass and have a general tidy up so that the police don't suspect that there's been any foul play. Then we'll have a look for stuff that nobody might know she had so they won't realize it's missing. Then tomorrow, you can contact the authorities and report a dead body. Deal?"

"Let's just do the tidying up first," said Nick, bending down to pick up the bedside lamp he had knocked over earlier. "You might as well put that other lamp on now, at least we'll be able to see what we're doing."

Rob switched on the other bedside lamp and began to untether the dead woman. He put all the items, which had turned out to be unnecessary in the end, back into his holdall. As Nick returned the lamp to its rightful place, he tried to switch it on, and said, "The bulb seems to have fallen out of this lamp when it fell over. Is it on your side?"

"I can't see it. Maybe it's gone under the bed."

Rob knelt down and lifted up the duvet. "Hello, what have we got here, then?" he said, as he pulled out a couple of shoe boxes. Both boxes were white and identical in size. A dark green plastic strip with embossed lettering, which had seemingly been home made using a Dymo Label Maker, had been stuck to each lid. One label read 'Jackie's Cash Bank' and the other, 'Jackie's Wank Bank.' Immediately drawn to the one which mentioned money, Rob opened that lid first. "Shit! Now you're talking," he said, lifting up handfuls of bank notes of various denominations. "I told you it was your lucky day. Let's just take this shoe box and get out of here. We'll have half each and I'll even let you keep the box."

"No, we can't do that. It'll be stealing from the dead," said Nick.

"She doesn't need it anymore, does she? Plus, what's a shoe box full of money doing there anyway? Only wrong 'uns keeps money under the bed these days? It's probably dodgy, that's why it's there."

"Maybe it's for her relatives."

"What relatives? Some relatives they are, if they can just leave her lying stone cold dead in bed on her own and not do anything about it. They don't deserve it. We'll be helping her out by not letting them have it, especially as it was us that found her, and you who is notifying the authorities. If it wasn't for us, she might have been lying here for weeks. Think of it as a sort of reward so that she can rest in peace."

"It just doesn't seem right."

"Alright, what would you have done if there wasn't anybody here and we found this box?"

"That's different."

"Of course, it's different. We would have taken this poor woman's money and when she'd come home from her holiday, or wherever she'd gone, and found it missing, she would have been distraught. Wouldn't that have bothered you? At least this way, we haven't upset her, and we've done her a right favour by tidying up the place."

Nick was becoming increasingly unsettled and said, "Don't you think this is immoral? That taking from people is wrong, that stealing is wrong?"

"Perhaps you should consider finding another profession, mate. I don't think you're cut out to be a burglar. What made you come along with me in the first place, if that's how you feel?"

"I was forced into it. I was desperate. I wanted to get my life back because it feels like it's been stolen from me, and this was my only choice. I assumed if I went along with it, it would make everything alright again. Nobody told me it was going to be like this. This isn't right. You do whatever you want. It's entirely up to you to make the correct decision, but I'm going," said Nick, as he walked serenely towards the bedroom door leaving Rob kneeling on the floor, slowly shaking his head.

"Fucking weirdo," Rob said out loud, once Nick had gone. Then out of curiosity, Rob turned his attention to the other shoe box and carefully lifted the lid. Inside the box were various pictures of men who looked vaguely familiar to him. He was wondering where he'd seen these people before, when it dawned on him that these were the same men he'd seen earlier. The ones in those pictures on the table in the pub. There was even a picture of that bloke Reg who the auction was for. This was all getting a bit too mysterious for Rob's liking. A cold shiver ran down his entire body and he could have sworn that the temperature in the room had dropped considerably. As soon as he got the impression that he was no longer alone, he decided to grab the shoe box containing the money and get the hell out of this place for good.

Nick continued to calmly walk past the cemetery, along the dark lifeless street, and only once did he glance back. It was just as Rob came crashing through the glass of the bedroom window, his body landing in a twisted heap on the ground below. Somebody was bound to hear that, he thought, and continued on his soul-searching journey into the unforeseeable night.

This Used To Be Paradise Row

It was one of those rare late autumn days when there was a clear blue sky and a much-desired sun had unexpectedly appeared. Not that this was really appreciated, or even barely noticed by Tom, who sat feeling alone and confused on that familiar bench in Clissold Park. He had far too much on his mind to care about the weather. Caroline had not long left, and he'd frantically needed to get out of the flat they'd once happily called home, but which now he absolutely despised.

Caroline couldn't detest it as much as he did, he thought, as it wasn't costing her anything anymore. She was as keen as him to sell it, though, mainly he guessed, because she needed the money. Once the place was finally sold, he could start a new life and perhaps block her from his mind for good, but in the meantime, he was stuck there. It was worse than being in prison, he imagined, as unlike a prisoner he had to pay the mortgage, all the utility bills and buy his own food. Prisoners didn't have to go to work either, and they probably had a better sex life than he did, he thought, allowing himself a rueful smile.

Tom still didn't know where Caroline was living as she wouldn't tell him. Just with friends she worked with, she'd said, nobody he would know. The only way to contact her was on her work number and he only did that when it was urgent. He yearned for the time when he would be able to phone her and say the flat had finally sold, but now, eleven months since they'd put it up for sale, they were still resentfully bound together. Apparently, according to the Estate Agents, 1993 was a buyer's market and it didn't help that they'd bought it in 1986 when it was a seller's market. In between they had somehow acquired something called negative equity. Tom decided he was certainly no property expert, and he would have to make his fortune some other way, though that particular Saturday was not the time to fathom how he was going to go about doing it.

Like all irreparably broken relationships, theirs wasn't always filled with regrettable sadness and powerless frustration. They'd both been extremely happy together for a number of years and then something, which Tom was also unable to understand, just seemed to disappear. Something they both knew would never return. Despite it now being over seven years ago, he could still remember vividly how excited they were when they went to view the flat together one Sunday afternoon. How they worked together as a team to give the impression that they were not going to be intimidated by the estate agent, even though they were still only in their mid-twenties and had never bought property before.

"And this part of Stoke Newington Church Street here, between Clissold Crescent and Clissold Road, was once known as Paradise Row, you know," the estate agent had said, in that way that all estate agents have a habit of speaking.

"So, it obviously used to be a lot nicer back then."

"Oh no, this is definitely an up-and-coming area, and I would say that this particular flat is probably the largest one-bedroom flat I have ever seen."

"Another estate agent said exactly the same thing to us yesterday about a completely different property."

"It would without doubt make a wonderful pied-a-terre."

"Does that mean we'll have to buy somewhere else as well as this then?"

"Anyway, there has been an incredible amount of interest in this property. Let me show you around. I've shown so many other people this place all weekend, that I could probably do it blindfolded."

"That sounds like fun, shall we try it."

"Also, do you know that Stoke Newington Church Street is the longest name for a street in the whole of North London? And I wouldn't be surprised if it was probably one of the longest in the whole of London as well."

"Does that mean we can get some money off it then? Considering it will take us longer to write the address when we fill out any forms."

They had put in an offer later that afternoon and when it was accepted, jumped up and down hugging each other, not caring at all that they were in the phone box just outside the Funeral Parlour, opposite Abney Park Cemetry. A few months later, once they'd fully settled in to their perfect home, they often, only part jokingly, used to say to each other that living there together really did feel like being in paradise.

Tom's mind then began to wander from the reverie of those happy times together, to those much later in their relationship which had tormented him. The nights he'd sat waiting by the telephone wishing Caroline would call, if only to say she wouldn't be coming home but that she was safe and well. The agony of not knowing what he should do tearing him apart. The fear of what he might find out haunting his mind and gnawing away at the emptiness of his hollow stomach. The confusion he felt when she did come home and whether to believe what she had told him. The shameful loneliness of not being able to share his problems with anybody. The invisible barrier that seemed to appear between them, making everything they once did instinctively together now seem unnatural. The constant distrust as he ransacked the conversations she had with him, analysing them over and over in his mind, searching for clues to give him the solution to a conundrum he was afraid to solve. The self-disgust he'd endured as he covertly went through the dirty washing basket when he was alone, checking her knickers for evidence of cum stains. If he had found any, he was certain they would not have been his, as they'd not had sex together for several weeks. Not because he hadn't asked. He'd asked many times. He always assumed that they used to enjoy sex together and desperately felt that if they could just get back to doing that again, everything could be resolved. Caroline had evidently not shared the same optimism.

Tom also embarrassingly recalled the letter he'd once written to Caroline, when he no longer was able to articulate what he genuinely wanted to express without turning into a tearful gibbering wreck. He'd spent a whole afternoon choosing his words carefully, as he was sure that it was his last shot at not losing her forever. He'd watched Caroline reading the contents of it in front of him when she arrived home later that night, hoping she would believe how much he honestly regretted previously saying that he wasn't sure he wanted to be in a relationship anymore. How he now realized how much he truly did love her, and how certain he was that he did want to have a child with her, after all. Caroline finished the letter, started to cry, and then without saying a word, slowly shook her head.

He'd been right about the letter being his last chance. The very next day, Caroline took some of her things and moved out. They agreed to put the flat on the market and Tom offered to take on the mortgage and pay all the bills for the short time they had expected it would take for the flat to sell. The longer it took, the more he grew to hate the place. He dreaded coming home to an empty flat, especially when it was cold and dark outside.

Weekends were the worst. He would go out on Friday evening and stay out for as long as there was somewhere to still carry on, or until it became physically impossible to continue, before returning home, usually around 1pm on Saturday afternoon, to fall in to bed unconscious. He would wake up on Saturday evening and go out and do it all again. Sleep it off Sunday afternoon before going out for a few hours on Sunday night. Once, after a particularly heavy session during the winter, which started on a Friday night and continued all the way through to Sunday morning, he'd awoken and looked at his watch all confused. Eventually he worked out that it was showing the time to be 6.30. Dragging himself out of bed he staggered across the room and looked out of the window. There was dense fog and an eerie silence everywhere. As it was pitch black outside, he had no way of knowing for certain if it was 6.30pm on Sunday or if he had slept all the way through to 6.30am on Monday. In a panic, he'd dragged his damaged body as fast as he could manage into the living room to switch on the TV for clarification and had never been so overjoyed to see that 'Songs of Praise' was on. Suddenly finding himself in seventh heaven, he'd promptly got himself together and then went out again, all the way over to south west London to somewhere in Parsons Green. A woman he worked with was having a drinks party and it had given him something to do and somewhere to go. That was the night when sitting on the night bus home, the tears unexpectedly began to stream down his face, mirroring the droplets of rain on the bus's ineffective window.

Last night had been quite different as Tom was fully aware that Caroline was coming round to the flat the following day in order to collect some urgent post. A letter had arrived, addressed to them both, from their insurance company. He'd opened it and was surprised to see that it referred to a recent telephone conversation regarding a lost woman's Cartier watch, the value of which was in the region of £500. This clearly alluded to the watch that he'd bought Caroline for her thirtieth birthday, almost two years ago. She hadn't mentioned anything to him about losing her watch, and he doubted that it was because she was being considerate and didn't want to upset him. He'd phoned her at work and remembered her getting quite irate that he had opened the letter. She arranged to come round and get the letter the following Saturday, sometime around mid-morning, and he'd agreed to be there to discuss the matter further.

As a result, Tom had sensibly gone straight home once the club he'd gone to on Friday night had closed at 6am. Not used to being home so early, he decided to fix himself a little night cap and also rack up another line of coke. He began to feel quite amorous and had visions of Caroline and himself making love together later that day. No, that was all wrong he decided. That wasn't going to happen. He needed to get that out of his mind and be rational. He then chose to focus on another image to assist in his self-pleasuring, but various images of women, some he'd met and some he hadn't, were all spinning around in his head, vying for the undivided attention he was at present unable to give. It was shortly afterwards that he remembered Caroline's Littlewoods catalogue in the magazine rack. He checked the index for the Women's Lingerie section, opened the magazine at the appropriate page, and hurriedly pulled down his trousers and pants. He knelt down in front of the various pictures, took his sad member in his hand and started to tug on it, furiously.

Tom had no idea how long he'd persevered, determined to bring the task in hand to a successful conclusion, but at some point, he must have abandoned the mission and collapsed face down on the living room floor, exhausted, leaving a variety of scantily clad models unabashedly on display.

Caroline still had her key to the flat and when she let herself in at eleven that morning, was more than a little surprised to find Tom in the position he was in.

"What the fuck is going on here?" she shouted at the prostrate, unconscious figure in front of her.

"Uh! What? Nothing." Tom exclaimed, as he tried to pull up his trousers and pants as quickly as possible, in the futile hope that Caroline hadn't noticed that he wasn't wearing them in the expected civilised fashion.

"You make me sick."

"I'm sorry. I must have fallen asleep. I've been working really hard lately," Tom explained, before seeing the Littlewoods catalogue and noticing, to his horror, that it was open at the Children's Underwear section.

"I can't believe I lived with a paedophile for all these years and didn't know it. Shit, I really am going to be sick," Caroline announced, running towards the kitchen and throwing up just before she got to the sink.

"Don't worry about that, I'll clean it up later," said Tom, in an attempt to hopefully defuse the situation.

"Is that all you've got to say?"

"No, of course not. Look Caroline, I honestly don't know how that happened. Maybe the wind blew the catalogue when you opened the front door."

"What? You expect me to believe that the wind blew my Littlewoods catalogue out of the magazine rack, while you were asleep on the floor with your trousers and pants round your ankles, and somehow just landed in front of you opened up at the Children's Underwear section?"

"No, I definitely already had it open, but it was at the Women's Lingerie section. A draft must have blown the pages over."

"And it just so happens that this imaginary draft blew it to that section did it and not to any other section? If you'd bothered to go out of the flat this morning, instead of lying around, spending all your time tossing yourself off, you'd know that it isn't even that windy outside."

"Look, can we just forget it, please?"

"What, forget that somebody I used to live with likes wanking himself off while looking at pictures of children in their underwear? I can't believe I used to let you touch me. Who else knows about this?"

"Nobody."

"You need help. Maybe we should call the police."

"Come on Caroline don't be stupid. You know me better than that. It was just a freak accident."

"Don't call me stupid. And if there's any freaks around here, it's you. I only came round to get my insurance form, anyway. I'm getting out of this place before all your mates from the paedophile ring get round here."

"Wait a minute, please. We need to talk. What happened to your watch, anyway? You didn't tell me you'd lost it."

"We're no longer together, remember? I don't have to tell you everything that's happened in my life."

"No, I know you don't. But I bought you that watch as a present and the insurance policy is still in both of our names, so I thought you might have mentioned it."

"Just give me the form, will you?"

"Tell me how you lost the watch first."

"It just got lost. If I knew how or where it got lost, I'd still have it wouldn't I?"

"I hope this isn't some dodgy claim because you need the money. If it is, my name is on the policy, and I'll get done for it as well."

"How many more times do I have to tell you? It's not a dodgy claim, alright? Anyway, if anyone's been doing anything dodgy round here, I think it might be you."

"Don't bring that up again. I know we aren't together anymore, but I bought you that watch as a special present."

"So, do you want the money back for it then?"

"No, of course not. I just thought, I don't know, that perhaps it might still mean something to you, that's all. Are you going to buy another one when you get the insurance money to replace it? If you did, that would absolutely mean the world to me."

"Why are you crying, Tom? It's only a watch."

Tom was unable to continue the argument. He turned away from Caroline, and with considerable difficulty as he fought back his sobbing, said, "The letter from the insurance company is over on the mantlepiece. You don't have to leave straight away, do you?"

"Yes, I've got to go. I've arranged to meet a friend for a Rum Punch Brunch, though I probably won't be drinking," replied Caroline, as she walked over to get the letter. "Goodbye Tom, and get some help, yeah?" she added, as she made her way towards the front door.

As Caroline opened the door, a sudden gust of November wind took the opportunity to invade the flat, briefly assaulting Tom's tear-stained face as he stood there feeling hopelessly exposed. He watched as the front door closed again, like a cell door, ensuring that he continued his sentence of inescapable loneliness, which, even after taking into consideration time off for good behaviour, was certain to last a painfully long time.

Tom looked down at the offending Littlewoods catalogue which was still lying in exactly the same place on the floor and noticed that the pages must have been blown over by the sharp breeze created when Caroline had left. It was now open at the Men's Underwear section. Impotent frustration caused him to sink to his knees in desperation. Tom decided to loosen his trousers yet again. "Oh well, maybe third time lucky," he said out loud to nobody at all.

Reservoir Decalogues

Lyle rose from the chair he had been sitting in. The time had come for him to leave the house and do what needed to be done. He set off in semi-darkness on the long walk, intending to put his restless mind at ease.

He made his way up Green Lanes to the old Victorian pumping station castle, and onto where the path that ran alongside the New River began. After walking for some time, Lyle stopped to look across the East Reservoir. He could sense the beginning of what was certain to be a beautiful mid-summer sunrise. After surviving the blackness of the night, he felt comforted by the orange glow of the unseen sun that was starting to turn the sky pink. So incredibly gorgeous, he thought, that it was enough to make some fortunate people feel glad to be alive. Lyle was relieved that everywhere was as peaceful as he'd hoped it would be at dawn on a Sunday morning. There wasn't even anybody jogging, riding a bicycle or taking their dog for a shit. Lyle sat down feeling a little overwhelmed by it all.

Lyle resumed his walk shortly after the first rays of morning sunlight had gently caressed his skin and given him a much-needed good morning kiss to set him on his way. He continued walking along the New River Path, a route he was all too familiar with. After reaching the end of the first part of the path, he crossed the unusually quiet road at the intersection between Amhurst Park and Seven Sisters Road, opened the narrow gate, and was back alongside the serene river once more. Once he had passed a small block of flats on the other side of the river, he was able to appreciate the solitude again. He looked at the empty warehouses and the tall, old industrial chimney on the far side of the riverbank and felt almost reassured in his loneliness.

Lyle's transient complacency was quickly shattered when he noticed the silhouette of something hooded and motionless in the distance. Whatever it was seemed to be staring directly at him. He stopped dead in his tracks, surprised at seeing the first living soul he had encountered that day. Determined to complete his mission, he continued walking along the path until he reached the mysterious figure.

"Where are you going at this time in the morning?" asked the figure in the light grey hooded top, matching jogging bottoms, and white trainers.

Lyle, who could now identify the figure as somebody who was probably in his late teens, replied, "I'm going for a walk. What's it got to do with you?"

"You're up early?"

"So are you."

"No, I'm not. I'm out late. I ain't been home yet."

"Good for you. You only get one shot at this, and life's too short not to enjoy yourself."

"Okay, let's try this again. Where exactly are you going?" said the teenager.

"I'm going straight up this path," Lyle replied.

"What's your postcode?"

"Why, have you got a delivery for me?"

"Alright Mister don't try and be smart," said the teenager. "Where do you live?"

"Stoke Newington. Why?"

"What gang are you in?"

"I'm forty-seven years old."

"Well, you're old enough to know your postcode then. Judging by the way you're dressed it's got to be N16. You're not in N16 now, you know. N16 is back there. This bit here is probably no man's land, but behind me is definitely N4. And my gang, The N4 Sirs, hate gangs from other postcodes. We don't want them in our territory. And you're about to come into our territory. If you come any closer, you'll be dicing with death."

"Look, I don't know what the fuck you're talking about," said Lyle. "I'm going for a walk. If you think I'm going to turn around just because I've gone into a different postcode, you are very much mistaken, my friend. Now, it's been very enlightening talking to you, but I need to be on my way."

"Alright, I'll let you through, but you've got to give me all your money first."

"Let me give you a friendly piece of advice, free of charge. Go home to your Mummy & Daddy or go and play with your stupid little gang friends. You really are picking on the wrong person this morning. I am not in the mood to be mugged and certainly not by you. So, I shall ask you very nicely. Please, kindly move out of the way and let me carry on doing what I need to do."

"I ain't a kid. I don't live with my parents; I live with my missus. For fucking God's sake, man, just give me your money or I will find out where you live, and I swear, I'll move into your house, fuck your wife and keep all your pets and possessions."

"I've had more than enough threats for one day, thank you. Are you going to move out of the way, or not?"

"Make it easy on yourself. You need to be clever here. Once you've given me all your money, you can go and enjoy the rest of your day and won't end up like that dead body in the river back there."

"What! You've found a dead body in the river, and you just left him there? Have you phoned the police?"

"No, I ain't a grass and it's not like it needed any help. I passed it a while ago."

"Show me exactly where he is. We need to call the police and report it right away, otherwise you'll be a prime suspect for murder."

"I didn't do it." exclaimed the teenager. "I don't know who did it. Honest, I don't. I just noticed it there."

"I know you didn't do it, and you know you didn't do it, but what if someone saw you earlier and identifies you to the police. It's going to look a bit suspicious if they find out you just left a body lying there in the river, isn't it? You know what that lot are like, don't you? They'll do anything to solve a case quickly and pin it on the first person they come across. If you report it, at least you'll be off the hook."

They walked the short distance further along the path together until they reached the dead body lying face down in the shallow river. A raft of ducks floated nonchalantly by, while on the other side of the riverbank, a gaggle of geese were curiously wondering how events were going to unfold.

"Call the police," said Lyle. "Let's get this over and done with."

"I don't know the number, you do it," replied the teenager.

Sometime later, Lyle finished his call to the emergency services, placed his phone back in his jacket, and slowly shook his head from left to right, sighing softly.

"What did they say?" enquired the teenager.

"They said to stay exactly where we are, not to touch the body, and they would send a pair of Special Constables down here to look into it and take our details."

"What do you mean by 'Special'? That they've been specially trained to deal with dead bodies in the river?"

"No, I doubt it."

"What like special needs, then?"

"No."

"Well, what, then?"

"Maybe somewhere in between the two. Special Constables are voluntary police."

"What? There's such a thing as voluntary police? You wouldn't get me doing that if you paid me."

"Whoever they are, they're not going to be here for a while, anyway. So, have you got anymore pearls of wisdom you'd like to share to pass the time?"

The teenager looked around and then stared up at the sky. After a short while, he asked, "Who do you support?"

"What, other than my wife and pets, you mean?"

"Yeah. What football team?"

"Why? Are you going to have a fight with me if it's different to the one you support? The whole world can't all support the same football team and live in the same postcode, can they? You do realize that by wasting your energy fighting these other people, who are the same as you, is just what the establishment wants? That way, you can't all unite as one and use that combined energy to overthrow the rich few who are controlling the poor miserable majority's exploited lives."

"Alright, mate, calm down. Who do you think you are, that fella Karl out of the Marx Brothers?"

"Okay forget it," said Lyle, shaking his head. "For what it's worth, Arsenal."

"Nice one, I knew deep down you were alright. That's my team as well. Do you go?"

"Not anymore. I had a season ticket for years, but I gave it up. I haven't been for a while."

"Do you think you'll ever go back?"

"Not even if Jesus himself came down to play centre-forward," Lyle replied. "It's not like it used to be. I don't feel part of it anymore. It seems to be all about commercialism these days. What about you?"

"No, I can't afford it."

The two men stood side by side in silence for a few minutes.

"Who's your favourite player?" asked the teenager.

"What?" snapped Lyle. "None of them. I've lost interest," he added, looking impatiently at his watch.

"Alright, who's your favourite player of all time?" said the teenager, with a smug look on his face.

"Now that is a really difficult question. Over the years I suppose it's been, Charlie George, Tony Adams, Ian Wright, Denis Bergkamp, Thierry Henry-"

"Oh mate, it's got to be Thierry. Thierry is God. He's even my mum's favourite player but that might be because she fancies the arse off him. She's always going on about her fantasies where she imagines Thierry coming round our house one day and giving her one. I told her, if she's not careful she's going to end up with Wanker's Cramp or Tosser's Elbow, or whatever the correct medical term is when you've been cracking one off too much."

"I'm not sure I really want to hear about your Mum's habits, if you don't mind. It's still a bit early in the day for all that. What does your dad say about it?"

"He doesn't seem to mind. I once saw him staring at a picture in the newspaper of Thierry. It was that one where he's got his socks pulled right up so that they look like he's wearing white stockings and you can just see a little bit of thigh below his shorts. The boring old fucker just sat there for ages looking a bit confused. Then he didn't say a lot for the rest of the day. I think that was the night he couldn't finish his dinner and went to bed early."

Before they had a chance to continue their conversation, they noticed two men in uniform approaching them along the path. Once the uniformed men had reached their destination, the older one wearing glasses spoke, "Good morning, Gentlemen. I'm Special Constable Windsor." He pointed towards his much younger colleague, and added, "And this is Special Constable Johns, who is usually assigned to Stratford, but today will be assisting me in this investigation. Now, first of all, apologies for keeping you waiting, but we've been tied up. Police affairs. I can't disclose any details as it's strictly private and confidential. Right, let's get down to business. Who discovered the body and at what time precisely?"

"We both did," said Lyle, before the teenager had a chance to open his mouth. "At exactly the same time."

"I see. So, you and your son were out walking together, and you came across the dead body over there?"

"No, we've only just met, and we were coming from opposite directions," Lyle replied.

"Hang on, there's something here that's bothering me," S.C. Windsor said, putting the palm of his hand to his forehead. "You've only just met your son, and it just so happens that on the morning you arrange to meet each other for the very first time, you come across a dead body in the river. That's a bit of an unfortunate coincidence, wouldn't you say?"

"He's not my son, I've got no idea who he is."

"That's right, I'm not his son and he isn't my dad," said the teenager. "We've got a lot in common. I don't know who that dead bloke in the river is, either. I've never seen him before. We've reported it, so can we go now?"

"Not so fast, Sonny Jim," S.C. Windsor replied, taking out his notebook and the remnants of a well-used pencil. "I need to take down your particulars first and I've got a few more questions for you both. In my experience, nine times out of ten, this is an open and shut suicide case. We get a lot of them round here. I really hope this isn't the exception to the rule. Today is my last day on the force and I was hoping for a nice, quiet shift. If we are talking about a murder here, it's going to play merry hell with my retirement plans."

"He's going to buy a boat and go fishing," said the younger Special Constable. "And he told me that I could go out with him one day."

"That's the plan, yes. Though not in this river or that reservoir back there, obviously. My wife, she said to me, 'Frank, let's get out of London and make the most of our last few years together. We should go and live somewhere that's friendly, safe, and beautiful. A place where there's no hatred or greed and everybody looks after one other.'"

"Where are you going to go then?" asked the teenager.

"I'm still looking, so she hasn't quite decided yet. Anyway, knowing my luck, this is bound to be a murder case. So, unfortunately, it'll probably be some time before I'll be inviting any of my old colleagues in the force to come on my boat, that's for sure." Turning to face Lyle, S.C. Windsor continued, "Sir, you haven't said much for a while, is there anything you'd like to share with me."

"Like what?"

"Like, what you are doing going for a walk round here, this early on a Sunday morning, looking, if you don't mind me saying so, suspiciously well dressed. How much did you pay for those shoes?"

"Enough. What do you mean?"

"You're not wearing sportswear like Sonny Jim here."

"I'm forty-seven years old. I don't want to wear sportswear. Is it a crime now to take pride in your appearance?"

"No of course not, it's just that you look like you might have been out all night, whereas Sonny Jim here has clearly just woken up and thrown on suitable attire for his early morning stroll. If you have been out all night, then it is very possible that you might well be a suspect in this murder case."

"How do you know he's been murdered? And if I had murdered him, why would I phone up the police to report it?"

"Ah, it's criminal psychology, isn't it? I've read a lot of books on the subject. My wife thinks there's something wrong with me. But I had to, you see, in order to get where I am today. Rule number one: the murderer always returns to the scene of the crime."

"Listen, Special Constable Windsor, I can assure you that if that man over there in the river was murdered, it wasn't me that did it. Now, can we go please?"

"One more question, sir, and it's a bit of a personal one if you don't mind. Was there anybody with you at any time last night?"

"No, I was all alone."

"What? I thought you had a wife and some pets," said the teenager.

"I did but somebody took them away from me," replied Lyle, before turning towards S.C. Windsor. "I wish I could help you more, I really do, but I can't. I think you're a doing an excellent job and I appreciate everything you're doing to make this area a much safer place. Your presence around here certainly makes me feel a lot more secure. I would even go as far to say that you personally, put the special and the stable into Special Constable."

"Thank you, sir. That's the nicest thing anybody's ever said to me."

Lyle turned to walk away, leaving S.C. Windsor scratching his head and staring solemnly at the dead body. What a fucking idiot, thought Lyle, thinks he's a detective but he can't even see a bluff when it's staring him right in the face.

Turning round, S.C. Windsor raised his right index finger, and said, "Just one more thing. You're not planning on going on any long journeys out of town are you sir? We might need to contact you again."

"No, don't worry. I won't even venture out of my post code," Lyle replied, heading back towards where he'd started his journey.

The teenager followed him and, once they were safely out of earshot of anybody else, said, "Thanks for not telling them that it was me who found the body first and wasn't going to report it."

"Don't mention it. The pleasure was all mine."

"So, what are you up to now? I suppose as it's Sunday morning and you're all dressed up you must be off to church."

"Church?" scoffed Lyle. "I don't think either of us would be very welcome in church. Between us, one way or another, I think we've already broken all their main rules today – and that's before most people have even woken up. Go home to your missus. You might not realize it now, but take it from me, one day you'll regret the time you didn't spend together and will wish you could have another chance to say all the things you never said."

Trial And Error

Jay was vacantly staring out of the window of the speeding train that was taking him from one place where he was not wanted, towards another that would not be welcoming him back. He couldn't quite read the names of the signs as they went flashing by, but the stations looked familiar enough to satisfy him that he would soon be arriving at Kings Cross station.

He'd just spent six months, to the day exactly, in a place called Berwick Upon Tweed, attempting to run a small BnB business. Love makes you do strange things and has a way of proving unequivocally, that you really are in love with somebody. It'd been something of an on / off relationship with Kay for around eighteen months, more off than on if he had to be honest. It'd been the most confusing and invigorating year and a half of his life, and whatever the official status happened to be at any particular time, his feelings towards her never changed.

Having previously always believed that the only way to get over a failed relationship was to completely stop seeing that person, he'd surprised himself by not adhering to that philosophy when it came to Kay. He wondered if it was because he was so in love that he just couldn't let her completely disappear from his life, even though he knew, deep down, that it was all bound to end miserably. Another possibility he'd considered for this unexpected turnaround in his strategy was that at no time had she actually uttered the words, 'Sling your hook,' 'You make me sick,' 'I really hate the sight of you' or 'I never want you to darken my door again,' as others had in the past, so that probably had something to do with it as well.

He'd been in love before, many times, but with Kay, it seemed so exceptional. It was almost as if it had come from outer space, entirely consuming him, and controlling every waking second of his life with thoughts of her. When he wasn't with her, he only wanted to be with her, and as soon as he was with her, he didn't want to be anywhere else.

Maybe he'd just forgotten how intense love could be, but there had definitely been something strange going on with him. So, when Kay had suggested, during one of their off periods, and just before an on one, that he come up and help her run a BnB in Berwick Upon Tweed, he immediately said yes.

From that moment they'd got on so well together. Though, like all happy relationships, there had also been times when one of them had wanted to throw the other out of the window. Fortunately, those occasions had been few and far between. They were both basking in the glory of taking control of their own destiny. Getting out of the London rat race, and no longer having to be wage slave prostitutes working for The Man. Neither of them had any experience in the hospitality industry, nor had they ever lived in Berwick Upon Tweed, but how difficult could it really be? Most importantly, they had each other, and love conquers all.

Once the train had pulled into Kings Cross, Jay got his suitcase down from the rack and made his way to the Underground. He'd already decided to get the Victoria Line to Seven Sisters, and then the Overground from there to London Fields. It was home. Somewhere familiar. Even though he had nobody to go to or anybody waiting for him, at least he wouldn't end up somewhere out of his comfort zone.

Trial And Error

Both trains Jay travelled on for the rest of his journey were quiet, allowing him to remain focused on his reflections.

Kay had found the place in Berwick Upon Tweed and said it was ideal. It was a house with a recently converted annex in the garden that could be used to accommodate paying guests. She'd bought the property and had told him to give up his tiny rented flat and move in with her. The money they would make from running the BnB would give them a decent standard of living without either of them having to work themselves into an early grave. It felt good being the furthest north they could possibly be without moving out of England. Not that you'd know you were in England. Most people didn't class themselves as English, saying they were Berwickers. Some, incredibly, even said they were proud to be Scottish. Whatever they were, they all took an instant dislike to him. It's the only place he'd ever lived where somebody had come up to him in the street and said, 'I don't know who you are, but I really don't like you.' He preferred the anonymity of London, all day long, any day of the week.

Even the old pensioner they employed as their handyman had tried to convince them one afternoon that they should leave immediately, maintaining that they were putting their lives in serious danger by living there. This was due to Berwick Upon Tweed still being officially at war with Russia. Something to do with the Crimean War, he insisted. Apparently, when war was declared on Russia in 1853, it was signed by 'Queen Victoria of Great Britain, Ireland & Berwick Upon Tweed.' Then, when the peace treaty was signed, three years later, someone forgot to include the 'Berwick Upon Tweed' bit. Stupid old twat, but when you're only paying somebody minimum wage to stick his hand down a blocked toilet to retrieve some stranger's enormous turd that's got stuck in the pan, then you pretend you're interested in what they've got to say. Up to a point.

Jay arrived at London Fields and decided that he could do with a well-deserved pint after the long journey and made his way to The Martin Amis. Although he hadn't set foot in the place for six months, he noticed that nothing in the pub had changed. It was still as dreary as ever with a smattering of ugly and tired losers, boozers, abusers and users. Desperate people who may have once tried to break free from their doomed existence but failed miserably and have now subserviently accepted their fate. A few sad and lonely people were staring into space, shell shocked by life, embarrassed to still be alive, having already surrendered to be taken prisoner in the great war of existence. People who have had their souls ripped out of them and know that they will never be reunited. Yes, he was certainly back home again.

Having ordered and paid for his drink Jay went and sat down at an empty table and listened to some of the conversations going on around him. The usual rubbish, everybody complaining about something or other and blaming somebody else. Their only visible talent being that they could do flawless impressions of people pretending to be boring idiots.

As Jay lifted his glass to take another sip of his drink, he noticed a woman walking towards him. She appeared to be in her late twenties or early thirties, smartly dressed in a black trouser suit and was relatively attractive.

"You don't mind if I sit here and talk to you, do you," the woman said, already sitting down and making herself comfortable.

"That depends. You're not a retard, a prostitute, or on the ponce, are you?"

"Why do you say that?" she laughed.

"Because they're the only people who usually come and talk to me for no good reason," he replied.

"No, don't worry. I'm none of those."

"Well, what are you doing in here, then?" he asked.

The woman laughed again without answering the question. She looked down at his suitcase and asked, "Have you been away? Anywhere nice?"

"I obviously forgot to include 'hairdresser' in that list."

"No, I'm not one of those, either," she laughed again. "I'm just trying to be friendly."

"Ah, so you're one of The Monkees."

"Excuse me? Look, if you'd rather be left alone, that's fine. I just thought you might like to talk, that's all."

"Sorry, I've had a really bad day. I didn't mean to be rude. Instead of me continuing to guess incorrectly, why don't you just tell me what it is that you do."

"You tell me why you've had a bad day first."

"Alright, if you're that interested, I will. It's a long story, but I'll try and make it quick and simple and leave out all the gory, deeply disturbing, emotional details. Six months ago, to the day, I moved up to Berwick Upon Tweed with somebody who I assumed was my girlfriend, to start a small BnB business. She told me last night, the day before her birthday, that she didn't think it was working out and that she wanted to do this all by herself. She owned the place, and I didn't have a say in the matter. So, I let her have her present and then I decided to disappear, and now I've come back to start my life all over again."

"I'm sorry, I shouldn't have asked."

"No not at all, don't worry, it's my own fault anyway. I shouldn't have jumped into it without a safety net. I gave up my job, my flat, my friends, my life, but hey, you live and learn."

"You trusted somebody because they obviously really meant a lot to you."

"You're right, she did mean a lot to me, and I trusted her. But I reckon she only wanted me to move up there just to help her settle in. I don't think it was even the standard six-month probationary period to see if I was up to scratch; I think she'd made her decision before we'd even got there."

"We all want and need somebody we can trust. Let's face it, there are more than enough people out there who we can't trust. That's why it's always so difficult to understand when somebody you believed in goes and betrays all of that."

"You're absolutely right, and it's really tough trying to make it through this world on your own. You shouldn't think that you will go through life never trusting anybody ever again just because you've had a terrible experience somewhere down the line."

They both sat in silence for a little while, deep in thought, thinking about things they wished had remained locked away in the cluttered attics of their minds. They were jolted from their personal melancholic trances by the sound of a bell ringing to signify last orders at the bar, and a man hastily falling over a chair in a desperate attempt not to be disappointed once again by the cruel, unforgiving world.

"Let me get you a drink, I can include it in the bill," the woman said, smiling and taking her purse out of her handbag. "What would you like?"

"I'll have a Brandy, please."

"Anything in it?"

"No, just straight."

"Okay. Coming right up, Mr Straight."

"As a die," Jay grinned, watching her calmly walk towards the bar.

The woman returned with the drinks, sat down and said, "So, have you got anywhere to stay tonight?"

"Why? Are you going to invite me back to your place?"

"No, I had no intention of doing that at all."

"I know. I was only joking," said Jay. "I'll probably stay in the Travelodge around the corner. It's unusual for a Travelodge to be busy on a Sunday night, so the prices are normally very reasonable. Then perhaps tomorrow, who knows, maybe I'll find myself a job, a wife and a home. A place where we can raise a family and live happily ever after."

"You're taking this very well, I must say. And you're definitely not the sort of person I was expecting to meet in here, at all," she said, finishing her drink. "Oddly enough, I do find you quite attractive as well, but perhaps you're just a little bit too old for me. Maybe under different circumstances, and if I was ten years older, I might give it a go."

"Okay, take my number and give me a call me in ten years' time," said Jay.

She smiled and stood up, "I'm sure I will see you again before then."

"I hope so. You haven't given me the check yet."

"The Czech is coming, you'll just have to trust me," she smiled, and walked out of the door.

"With my life," he said, taking another sip of his drink.

* * *

As soon as he was in his deceptively familiar room at the Hackney Travelodge, Jay undressed and got into bed. Here in the dark, with the duvet pulled right up to his forehead, he felt safe. In this sacred, brief moment in time, nothing could harm him. The world, with all of its horrors, would be able unable to find him here. Just as he was attempting to clear his mind for a final launch into deep sleep, he heard the sound of his door being unlocked.

"Hello?" Jay shouted. "No, it's okay. I don't need the room cleaned at the moment, thank you. Can you come back later, please?"

The door opened and the light was switched on, confusing him further with its harsh brightness. Two men dressed identically in black suits, white shirts and blue ties stood looking at him.

"Who are you and what the fuck are you doing in my room?" Jay enquired.

One of the men, who appeared to have an Eastern European accent, spoke, "Get dressed quickly, you fucking cockroach. You're coming with us."

"What for?"

"You know," said the other one, who was shorter and had a similar accent.

"Are you by any chance Russians?" asked Jay. "Because if this has got something to do with the war, I don't live in Berwick Upon Tweed anymore. But I'd be more than happy to tell you everything I know about the place."

"No, we are not Russians," the taller one said.

Jay got out of bed, and said, "What if I don't want to go with you?"

"If you would like to keep your private parts in their present position, you will come quickly," said the shorter one, whose turn it now was to talk.

Jay hurriedly began to get dressed. "Can't you just tell me what all this is about?"

Neither man answered as they handcuffed Jay and forcibly escorted him out of his room, down the stairs, and past the deserted reception area. He was able to glimpse into the back room behind the front desk and could see the amiable young man who had told Jay with great pride that today was his first day at work when he'd checked him in a short while ago. He'd been tied to a chair, blindfolded, and stripped down to his vest and underpants. His mouth had been crammed full of print-out receipts, and it was evident that he'd been crying and had soiled himself. Jay wondered just how much torture this young receptionist had endured before finally giving these men Jay's room number once he could take no more.

A black car was parked outside the Travelodge. The two men bundled Jay into the back of the car and sat down on either side of him. Jay noticed that the person in the driver's seat was the woman he'd been talking to earlier in the pub.

"I told you I'd see you again," said the woman. "Now where would you rather be taken, Hackney Marshes or The Castle on Green Lanes?"

"What for?"

"You already know," the taller man said, punching Jay in the stomach and temporarily winding him.

"I'm sure, like everybody else, your preference would be The Castle," said the woman, "but as you know, it'd be difficult to get in there, so let's go to Hackney Marshes. Not only is it more isolated, it's also a bit nearer. I won't use as much petrol, so it'll work out cheaper for you, as well."

The car drove off and once Jay was able to get his breath back, he said, "Look, I'm sorry but I really don't know what all this is about, can't you just explain to me what is going on?"

This time the shorter man punched him in the stomach. Jay saw a flash of orange and felt something surge up into his mouth. Afraid he would be sick, he swallowed whatever it was from the meal deal he'd had on the train earlier back down to where it had come from. His eyes welled up with tears for the second time that day.

"Stop asking questions, you're wasting our time," said the taller man. "Why are you pretending you don't know what is going to happen?"

As the car passed Mabley Green, Jay considered how he could find out what all this was about without asking any further questions. Eventually, all he could come up with was, "I honestly don't know what is going to happen."

"That's very good," said the woman, as she parked the car in a deserted road. "I like the way you're keeping up the pretense, it makes it a lot more interesting for us. All the others just stay silent, resigned to their destiny."

Everybody got out of the car. The woman led the way into Hackney Marshes, followed quickly by her two colleagues, who each had an arm under one of Jay's armpits. Once they'd reached a secluded spot on the banks of the River Lea, they stopped. The two men pushed Jay down towards the ground so that he was now on his knees. The taller man took out a large knife from the contents of the supermarket bag for life he was carrying and wore a smile on his face, implying that this was the part of his job he enjoyed the most.

The woman pulled out a piece of paper from her handbag, and said, "In accordance with your instructions, you have requested that we recognize you as being monstrous vermin and that we kindly put you out of your misery. This is because you no longer

Trial And Error

accept your own humanity and continue to deny your guilt. You have lost all hope of ever achieving happiness in this world and have finally accepted that life is the futile pursuit of an unattainable goal. Your chosen method of death is to be killed with a butcher's knife and to die like a dog. But not before you've had numerous apples thrown at you for being a massive dung beetle."

"I didn't request that," pleaded Jay. "I don't believe any of that at all. There's obviously been some kind of mistake here."

"Oh no, don't tell me we've got the wrong person, again," said the woman. "It must be another clerical error. I thought something wasn't quite right when I first met him. Let's get him back to his room in the Travelodge. Check out isn't until 12, so he can still get his money's worth. Come to think of it, as it's the same price for one as it is for two, I might as well go and spend the night there with him. It's my day off tomorrow."

Shed

"This is the life," Tony said out loud to himself as he sat in his garden. It wasn't a particularly beautiful garden, but it was satisfying enough and all his. It was a pleasant early summer's day, and that was all his as well now that he was happily retired. I can do whatever I want, whenever I want, with nobody to tell me what to do, when to do it or where to go and do it, he thought.

This was his first real day of retirement, having finally finished his working life on the previous Friday. The weekend had been spent as usual, with the only exception being that he didn't suddenly have a feeling of dread come over him early on Sunday evening. He'd been eagerly anticipating this particular Monday morning. Definitely the first and only Monday morning, that wasn't a holiday of some description, that he'd ever looked forward to, and he was determined to enjoy it. The only problem was, what to do first? He was spoilt for choice. He'd already spent far too long having his breakfast and reading the newspaper, before the bright summer sun had eventually smothered him in guilt and forced him out of bed. Never one for watching TV at the best of times, he certainly wasn't going to see what sort of rubbish is broadcast at this time in the day for the brain-dead, unemployable masses. It was still too early to put on some music and completely enjoy it. Watching a film at 10am just wouldn't feel right either. He eventually settled on simply sitting in his garden and reading a book.

I've earned this, he convinced himself, as he stretched out on one of his garden chairs. I've worked fifty odd years since leaving school. That's half a century and I hated every minute of it. I only did it to survive and luckily, I've got a decent pension, some savings and I've still got my health to be able to enjoy myself now. No more putting up with all that rubbish you have to for eight hours a day, five days a week. Having to constantly work alongside people who, given the choice, you wouldn't want to spend more than two minutes with in a lifetime. Stupid, boring, horrible people with bad breath and dreadful body odour. Fighting your way on to packed tube trains every morning at Manor House Station, just to make sure you get to work on time, and then have to do the same thing every evening at Bank Station, in order to get back home as quickly as possible so you can try to become yourself again. All those ridiculous rules and regulations you had to endure just so you could earn your miniscule yearly salary increase. (That's if you were lucky and even got one at all.) Goodbye and good riddance to all that, it's time to look forward to the future.

The future scared Tony though. It was entirely unknown, and he was also spoilt for choice. He'd spent the past year going over potential plans in his mind, hoping to have everything all arranged and ready for the big day. Perhaps if he knew exactly when he was going to die it would all be a lot easier. That way he could work out exactly how much money he needed every year and could go off and really enjoy himself without fear. It wasn't like he had any dependents to worry about leaving his money to anymore. Tony's wife Sandra had died after a long illness, on New Year's Day, four years ago and their only son, Jonathan, had died in a car crash while out celebrating his eighteenth birthday. There wasn't a day that went by when he didn't think of them or miss them both terribly. Sometimes, Tony wished he could believe in a religion and then he could look forward to seeing them again one day, but he knew deep down that that was never going to happen.

Unable to concentrate, he put his book to one side. A melancholic feeling had now engulfed him, and it was proving to be a lot harder to shake off than those he usually had. It's probably because I haven't got to concentrate on anything else, he assumed, I need to do something to occupy my mind. I really don't want to be one of those people you hear about who can't enjoy their retirement and wish that they were back at work. I've been looking forward to this since the first day I started working, so I'm going to make the most of it. I suppose I never really thought I'd be on my own when I retired, and I'm sure I'd feel a lot different if Sandra and Jonathan were still alive.

The last thing I want is to feel like this every morning, Tony thought. Perhaps I should sell up and get out of London. Make a whole fresh start. But where to? There's a whole world out there – I'm spoilt for choice yet again. I'm not sure I love London, or Hackney in particular, as much as I used to. I would never have dreamt of living anywhere else before, but now there's no reason for me to still be here. Maybe I should just go on a holiday first before making any rash decisions. But where though? Sandra always chose where they should go.

Tony began to recall some of the happiest times they'd had on holiday. There was the honeymoon when they'd spent those few days in Brighton. Sandra always said they must go back there one day, but they never did get round to it. Silly really, it's only down the road but I suppose when somewhere is so close, you always think you can go there any time you want.

Then there was the first time they had gone abroad. A couple of years after they were married and before Jonathan was born.

Those incredible evenings as they walked hand in hand along the promenade in Malaga just as the sun was setting. They had never seen sunsets like it. They were both transfixed by how beautiful the world could be and, this time, they did return, about six or seven years later when Jonathan was a small boy. It was still as lovely, but it wasn't quite the same though, as on this occasion they knew exactly what to expect.

They couldn't afford to travel abroad too many times after that, but he and Sandra did go to Venice for a long weekend, shortly after Sandra had been diagnosed. That certainly couldn't be classed as one of the happiest times, though. Tony's predominant memories of that trip were of them both trying to convince each other that they would fight this and get through it, whatever it took. He'd vowed to himself that he would stay strong for Sandra's sake, but he now embarrassingly recalled how he'd finally broke down in tears on that last afternoon, shortly before they were due to travel back home and start the treatment. A dreadful time ahead of them which would eventually turn out to be a losing battle. They had been on the Rialto bridge, and it was Sandra who'd ended up having to comfort him as the hordes of staring tourists walked by. She'd stopped him from crying by saying 'It's alright, everyone will assume that you must have bought a cup of coffee for us both in St Mark's Square and then went on a gondola.' He had to laugh. Sandra always made him laugh, even when her jokes weren't particularly original or even that funny.

Thinking about it, Tony realized he'd never laughed so much before meeting Sandra and so little after she'd gone. Although he was smiling at some of those unforgettable memories, tears were streaming down his face. He quickly got up and went back into the house to dry his eyes.

Right, I need to do something to keep myself occupied, Tony decided. It's all a bit too much to take in on my first day of freedom. A bit of a shock to the system. I should try and gradually ease into it. I can't sort the rest of my life out on the first day. I'll do something I can focus on to take my mind off everything else. Something relaxing, like gardening.

Tony changed into his gardening clothes, went back outside and walked towards the small shed at the end of the garden where he kept his tools. He unlocked the door, grabbed the handle and pulled it towards him. Strangely, the door seemed to draw back. He tried again, and then a third time, but the outcome was the same. Something must be caught and is getting in the way, he assumed. On his next attempt, he hauled the door handle with all of his strength, and the door finally opened, revealing an agitated looking young man who was standing there naked, holding a hammer above his head.

Tony, who had fallen backwards during the preceding struggle to open the door, and was now lying flat out on the ground, said, "Wait! I'm not going to hurt you."

The man stood there looking confused.

Tony slowly rose to his feet and raised both of his hands to show that he meant no harm to the intruder. "What are you doing in my shed without any clothes on?" he enquired.

"Hiding."

"Okay. But why are you naked? If you don't mind me asking."

"It's a bit warm in there."

"Alright, fair enough. Who are you hiding from?"

The man did not bother answering and instead began shielding his eyes from the bright sunshine as he tried to take in the surroundings.

"Why don't you put the hammer down, get dressed and come out of the shed," said Tony, more calmly than one would expect of someone who was being confronted by a naked man brandishing a hammer. "Then we can sit down and see what we can do to help you get, whatever it is, all sorted out."

"Don't call the police?"

"Let's just talk first and see what needs to be done. I promise I won't contact the police unless you decide that's what you want me to do."

"You mustn't call the police."

"Okay, no police."

"How can I trust you? How do I know you're not lying?" said the man, rapidly moving his head from left to right and staring intensely in both directions.

"Because I'm not going anywhere and I won't move out of your sight," Tony answered. "We can just talk, and you can tell me all about why you are hiding in my shed. It might make you feel better if you share your problems with somebody, and, you never know, I might even be able to give you some advice."

"About what?"

"About what you might be able to do, so that you don't have to hide anymore."

"In your shed, you mean? That's what you're really bothered about, isn't it?"

"Well, to be honest, I can't really say I want a naked man, or any man come to that, hiding in my shed. But I would like to help you out, if possible, so that you don't feel like you need to go and hide somewhere else."

"Alright. But don't move."

The man turned around and quickly gathered a small pile of clothing that was lying on the floor of the shed. Without leaving the shed, he began to clumsily dress into a pair of underpants, a t-shirt, a pair of jeans, socks and trainers, not once letting go of Tony's hammer.

"Can I get you anything," asked Tony. "Something to eat or drink?"

"No. Stay where you are, so I can see you."

"How did you get in to my shed, anyway? It was locked. And how long have you been hiding in there?"

"I arrived sometime during the night. I didn't need to unlock it. Even if I did, I've got the exact same key for this shed."

"You must be thirsty or hungry, aren't you?" asked Tony, hoping that if he gave this man something to eat and drink, perhaps he would leave him alone. The sooner he could get rid of him the better.

"I can't leave the shed, it's too risky and I don't trust you not to call the police."

Tony stood there, not really sure what he should do or say next. This man was clearly in some sort of trouble, but it didn't look like it was going to be easy to help him. Maybe the man will talk once he feels a bit more relaxed.

"I'm just going to get a chair from back there," said Tony. "Then we can sit down and have a nice chat and see if we can't sort this all out for you."

When Tony returned with one of his garden chairs, the man waited until Tony had sat down before he lowered his body sideways to the ground, resting his back against the frame of the shed door, all the while clutching Tony's hammer. The two men sat quietly looking at each other wondering who should start talking first. In the end, Tony decided he would break the uncomfortable silence.

"Okay, I'm Tony, by the way," Tony announced, although the man offered no acknowledgement and continued to gaze around the garden. "I take it you must be in some sort of danger."

"What makes you think that?"

"Just a wild guess, I suppose. Are you?"

"Not really."

Tony had never expected this to be easy, but he was beginning to think that perhaps he was a little out of his depth. Unable to come up with an alternative solution, he continued, "Okay, so if you aren't in any danger, why do you need to hide?"

"I'm waiting."

"Can I ask what for?" Tony asked, relieved that he didn't have an urgent appointment later that day.

"To be taken back."

"I see. To where, exactly?"

"The future."

"The future?"

"Yes, the future."

"How did you get here?" asked Tony.

"I was sent here."

"Okay, bear with me a minute while I get this straight," said Tony. "You've been sent from the future and somehow landed in my shed. Did whoever it was that sent you specifically want you to go to my shed?"

"Yes."

"If it isn't a stupid question, can I ask why?"

"To put things right."

"In my shed? What's wrong with my shed?"

"Nothing. The shed is alright, it's more about putting things right in the garden."

"Alright," Tony sighed, "What needs to be corrected in my garden?"

"Everything. But they sent me back a few hours too early, so I have to wait. They might even call me back to try again later and save a bit of time. I doubt it though, but I can't be certain."

"How long have you got to wait? asked Tony.

"What time is it now?"

Tony looked at his watch, "10.56," he replied.

"Only another fifteen minutes," said the man. "Are you okay to wait that long?"

"Yes, sure. I've got all the time in the world," Tony smiled. "So, tell me, while we wait, what's it like in the future then?"

"You wouldn't like it. It's a disgusting, violent place where everybody just looks out for themselves, takes whatever they can get from people without caring at all about anybody else."

"It sounds awful."

"It is, that's why they've invented time travel. They are sending everybody back in time to a moment where that person did something wrong in a particular place and have told everyone to make sure they do the decent thing this time and put things right. The name of the campaign is called, 'Correct the Past and Give a Present to the Future' The whole world is talking about it."

"And once everybody has put all these things right?"

"The future will automatically become a nicer place, of course."

"I see. So, assuming what you're telling me is true, and time travel really does exist, why hasn't anybody come back before?"

"Because they've only just invented it. It's still in its infancy stage. That's why I got sent back a few hours too early and had to wait in the shed. They can't go forwards into the unknown future yet either, so nobody knows if this is actually going to work. My generation are the pioneers of backwards time travel and the saviours of the future."

"Aren't you worried about not being brought back to your own time?" asked Tony. "Especially as this new invention seems to have a few teething problems."

"No. That's one thing that it is good at. As long as I stay in the shed, I will end up back in exactly the same time and place I was in before I was sent here. Which is back in my shed all over again."

"Your shed? Hang on, you're making my head hurt. Are you telling me that in the future this is your shed? Is this your garden as well? And your house?"

"Yes."

"How far in the future?"

"They sent me back six months from my time."

"What? Now you really are doing my head in," said Tony. "You're telling me that in six months' time, not only will you be living in my house but that's when they, whoever they are, manage to invent time travel?"

"Only backwards time travel, and no more than just enough future time travel to get you back to the present. Yes."

"And you really expect me to believe this rubbish?" laughed Tony.

"Yes, it's the truth."

"That somebody from six months in the future has come back to put something in my garden right that happened at, what time did you say?"

"Eleven-eleven."

Tony looked at his watch and said, "You've still got a good few minutes yet. So, answer this for me. Once something has happened in time, surely it can't be changed. It has been cemented in time forever. You can never alter what has already taken place."

"Well, this is what this campaign hopes to disprove. Like I said, it is early days yet, so at the moment it's all a bit of a step into the unknown."

"But it isn't though, is it? Not for you. If you're telling me the truth, then you know exactly what has already happened and may, or may not, happen again in a couple of minutes time."

"I do, yes. At eleven-eleven precisely on June 2nd, I bludgeoned you to death with your own hammer because you were going to call the police after you found me hiding in your shed. You told me some lie that you were going to get me a drink of water and make me a sandwich, but I didn't believe you. I ran after you and hit you right on the back of the head with the same hammer I'm holding now. You fell down and your whole body was twitching uncontrollably. You called out a woman's name, but I can't remember which one. I stood over you, and watched you die. You made a right mess as well. There was a lot of blood. It took me ages to clean it up."

The man paused briefly, before using the hammer to point towards the patio, behind where Tony was sitting. "And then I buried you under there and moved into your house." he said, getting up off of the floor. "Today, of course, I'm really going to have to try and not do that."

Confused and frightened, Tony quickly stood up. "Hang on a minute. Wait. Today's date is Monday 1st June," he said.

"Oh, you're joking," said the man. "Those idiots have sent me back a whole day earlier, not just a few hours. Do you mind if I wait in the shed? They might call me back. Anyway, I'll see you tomorrow, about the same time."

Tony stood watching as the man went back into the shed, closed the door behind him, and promptly disappeared.

Printed in Great Britain
by Amazon